Entangled Objects

Entangled Objects

A Novel in Quantum Parts

SUSANNE PAOLA ANTONETTA

ENTANGLED OBJECTS
A Novel in Quantum Parts

Copyright © 2020 Susanne Paola Antonetta. All rights reserved. Except for brief quotations in critical publications or reviews, no part of this book may be reproduced in any manner without prior written permission from the publisher. Write: Permissions, Wipf and Stock Publishers, 199 W. 8th Ave., Suite 3, Eugene, OR 97401.

Slant
An Imprint of Wipf and Stock Publishers
199 W. 8th Ave., Suite 3
Eugene, OR 97401

www.wipfandstock.com

HARDCOVER ISBN: 978-1-7252-5202-8
PAPERBACK ISBN: 978-1-7252-5203-5
EBOOK ISBN: 978-1-7252-5204-2

Cataloguing-in-Publication data:

Names: Paola Antonetta, Susanne.

Title: Entangled objects : a novel in quantum parts / Susanne Paola Antonetta.

Description: Eugene, OR: Slant, 2020

Identifiers: ISBN 978-1-7252-5202-8 (hardcover) | ISBN 978-1-7252-5203-5 (paperback) | ISBN 978-1-7252-5204-2 (ebook)

Subjects: LCSH: Fiction -- literary. | Korea -- Fiction. | Man-woman relationships -- Fiction. | Reality television programs -- Fiction. | Cloning -- Fiction.

Classification: CALL PS508.I73 E58 2020 (print) | PS508.I73(ebook)

Manufactured in the U.S.A.   JULY 20, 2020

For Bruce and Jin, my dearest entanglements

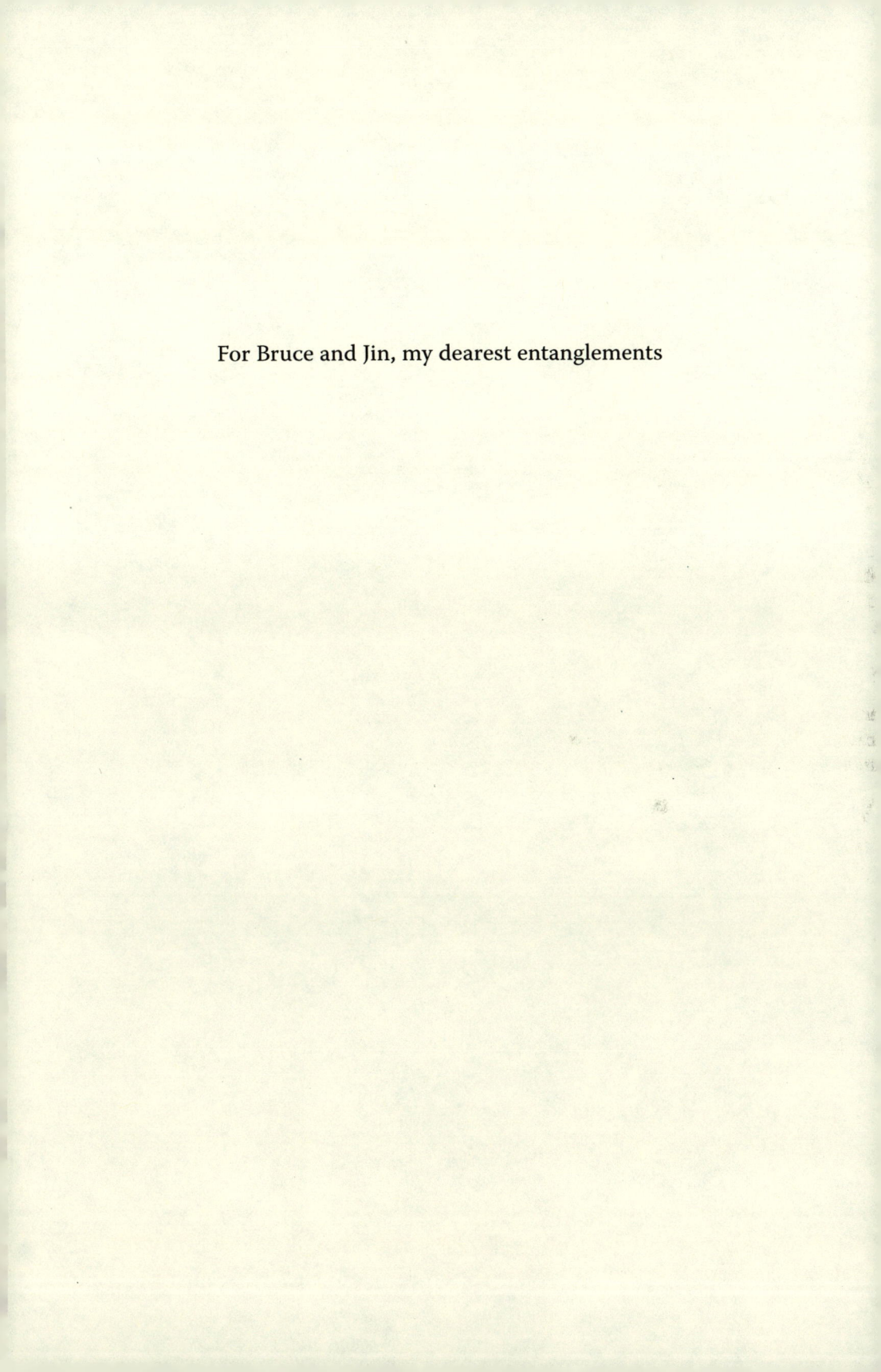

Contents

Part I
Fan: Spooky Action at a Distance | 3
Ef: Theft | 20
Fan: Loving a Calf as Well | 33

Part II
Ef: This Ordinariness | 55
CC: Copy Cat | 73
Fan: "Farewell, Good Ha Ha Ha" | 88

Part III
Fan: What Comfort to This Great Decay May Come | 103
Cate: Something Powerful Beyond Measure | 125

Part IV
A Butterfly's Wings | 133

Author's Note | 155
Acknowledgments | 157

PART I

Fan: Spooky Action at a Distance

Paul traveled to Korea in order to make a woman.
 Or at least that's how Fan put it to people who'd asked her. Sometimes, to punctuate the joke, she called him "Dr. Frankenstein" or "Victor." Or "Pygmalion," after the Greek sculptor who fell in love with his statue, then petitioned Aphrodite to bring her to life. Paul's new partner, In-Su, had successfully cloned a human female for the stem cells and planned to do it again. South Korea was particularly interested in therapeutic cloning, cloning humans for stem cells which, ideally, could be made pluripotent, or able to form duplicates of any cell in the body. There were good research funds.
 The female would just be an embryo, but the cells came from women, so it would be, technically, a woman. A lame joke, really, but Fan kept making it.

Now she sat in her apartment in Hongdae, a few weeks after their return to Korea. It was a two-bedroom, a large apartment in cramped Seoul, in a kind of building Koreans called officetels—skyscraper-y office-like buildings that had short- and long-term housing, gyms, and some businesses. It was an unusually large apartment for an officetel, and one the university kept for special visitors. Like most Korean homes, hers had heat that came up through the floors, beds low to the ground, an impossible washing machine the landlord recommended she watch a YouTube video to figure out, and no oven.
 Paul thought she would hate all these aspects of their place. In fact, she only hated the impossible washing machine. She loved the *ondol*, the heated floors, the way her body warmed from the soles up; she could swear she'd never been truly warm before. She loved the steel-and-glass

seriousness of her building. And she loved having no oven the way she loved many of the people she saw every day having no English—it took something she realized she'd never really wanted out of the daily equation.

Publicly as well as privately, she called Paul Victor rather than calling him by his name. Or she called him Pygmalion, though her tone was something neither of them fully understood. He simply called her Babe.

Yoon, the wife of her husband's new colleague In-Su, had given her brochures, things to do to entertain herself. She sat in the living room of her apartment and leafed through them, wondering.

"I want you to get out," Paul said every night after the lab. "Go to that spa, maybe. If you're intimidated by the subway, cab it." By *spa* he meant bathhouse, a place recommended by Yoon. Paul had trouble getting through his days without feeling Fan's days satisfied her. Fan sometimes pulled a certain facial expression when Paul fretted: mouth curved up a little, eyebrows raised a little, quietly optimistic. She started to pull it now but stopped.

"The one time I went to a spa in the U.S. I wanted to kill myself." Not that Paul didn't know. "All these people telling me I could've been a hand model." She picked up her left hand with her right and swung the fingers through the air. "'Those fingers! Sooo elegant!' I really just wanted to shoo them out and clean the tables. Clorox, Victor, Clorox."

"You feel like you don't deserve it," said Paul.

"That's not it. Who feels better about life because of their fingers?" Fan looked at her fingers, nails still a little mooned with garden grime. "They just need to flatter you. It feels so fake."

"You miss teaching?"

"The classroom has gotten boring. I appreciate the time off. I can refresh a little."

"Ah," said Paul. "You can do some reading, go over your syllabuses here, jazz things up."

"I guess." Had she given him what he needed to end this conversation?

"I'm happy, Victor," she said, knowing that he wouldn't understand the appeal of this stillness.

No matter what Fan said, Paul wanted to think she loved her job. Fan taught as adjunct faculty, a second-tier worker, not expected to publish, underpaid. She taught mostly Shakespeare courses and sometimes fiction. She was paid $3,900 per course and got health insurance if she taught four or more courses per year, but she had Paul's insurance, so it didn't matter. She earned little most years—well under $25,000—and if she had ever been competitive for a tenure-track teaching job, she was not any longer. She had published two stories in a decent but not highly selective literary journal, and never published any criticism, not even parts of her dissertation.

Her adviser in her doctoral program talked her out of writing a dissertation on Shakespeare, her great literary love, on the grounds that so many Shakespeare scholars existed the move was career suicide. So she wrote a dissertation on doubling motifs in the work of Thomas Kyd, a Renaissance playwright she got heartily sick of by the time she finished her PhD (it didn't help that he only wrote one identified play, *The Spanish Tragedy*).

She had not got much out of the process but an inner voice that boomed out Kyd lines like *farewell, good ha ha ha* at random moments. And, in an irony Shakespeare himself would have appreciated, she failed to find a tenure-track job, and wound up teaching Shakespeare, for a handful of coin, anyway.

The only way in which her education gave her a certain standard of living was, sadly, that it enabled her to marry Paul. He loved her but would not have fallen in love with a woman who had no standing within the academic world. Or one whose standing was equal to his, though he observed careful civilities about her work. She knew this about him, as she knew that a part of her love attached to the comfort that came with his money.

She wondered: if she had pursued Shakespeare, which she really loved, or gone after fiction, getting a degree in that and trying harder to publish, would things have worked out differently? She met her husband at the university, and he had tenure, plus a lab for his work.

Perhaps she had given Paul enough. *Own your authority*, he often told her about her teaching. Perhaps he'd imagined he heard something he could call owning.

Paul had grown up with money, and now had more. As a cloner, he did work in the agricultural sector, cloning sheep and cattle. What he earned varied, always within the six-figure range.

"Paul makes gu' money," as Fan's father put it, meaning *good money*. Her dad said *gu' money* about a lot of people's earnings. Once as a little girl she asked him what that meant. He said, Gu' money is what anybody makes who makes more than me.

Fan grew up in the Appalachian part of Pennsylvania. Her family mined coal. Neither of her parents finished middle school. Her father went from the mines to work as a machinist. Early in her life, there were times when they had cereal for dinner, always the sweet kind with pastel bits.

Fan would arrange the colors in her bowl: baby blue in the center, a circle of pink around it, then the boring tan ones. Sometimes they had odd combinations of food from the Food Bank—once a block of American cheese, canned beef stew, canned corn. Fan's mother, in what Fan took as a sort of protest, mixed these things into one dish. The cheese, probably more of a Velveeta than a real cheese, formed a molten blob in the center of the stew, and the corn floated. Once again Fan became obsessed with the aesthetics of her plate, swirling the stew around the cheese, the corn kernels moving fast and on top, like the bodies of Olympic swimmers. Both of her parents understood this stirring-staring as another form of protest. It was not.

Fan got ahead in life, went to school, working as a maid at a hotel. And she'd come to like that work in many ways, a fact that bothered Paul. He wanted her to hire a cleaning lady. She secretly loved cleaning the house, if she was in the mood, especially white surfaces like tubs. The sprays that made them shimmer. She might at times need to vee-fold the ends of a newly unwrapped roll of toilet paper. And then she'd hate to use it to wipe herself, so she'd hold in her pee for a while.

Unlike her, Paul loved his work. He loved to talk about it, not just the hope but the grotesqueries of animal cloning: the gigantism so extreme host mothers could die giving birth, the hundreds of deformations and deaths among the clones that preceded success, the aging that made Dolly the cloned sheep like a twelve-year-old at the age of three. She understood the basics, like how most of the quirks in cloning came from gene expression, not just what genes were present in the clone but whether they got turned on or turned off, so, for instance, the first cloned cat, named CC for Copy Cat or Carbon Copy, turned out a striped tabby, though her genes came from a cat that was calico.

Paul brought home photos to show her: a cloned calf with an enlarged heart that looked like a catcher's mitt; newborn creatures otherwise normal but with massive heads, so a newborn calf body sprawled under a head almost the size of a grown cow's; pig livers huge and bulbous with fat; swollen tongues jutting from tiny heads, as if the creatures had been hung.

Fan loved animals and wondered why Paul's work did not bother her more. Most of the photos were from other cloners' projects. They did not trouble her, though, even if Paul had a hand in the process, and her feeling was that in making a thing you got a free pass: it could be botched, like the play within a play in Kyd's *Spanish Tragedy*, a silly scene with a drama performed at court in which every character theoretically spoke a foreign language, though the characters just spoke English and pretended not to understand each other. The botch of the making showed the maker's hand.

"It's the newest medieval thing going," she said to Paul about cloning, and it became a joke for them. "Want to hear the newest medieval, Babe?" he said when he came home from work. Until Seoul: here when she asked him what the Middle Ages had produced that day, he shrugged.

"Oh," she said. "It's people, isn't it. I guess that's different." He didn't answer, merely watched her.

Fan for now just concerned herself with loving her freedom and with physics. Introduced to physics by Paul, she had come to understand it far better than he did. The concepts at least, not the math. She joined the British Institute of Physics one day, kind of a gag, but also serious. She selected her membership title from a very British pull-down menu: *Professor Dame*.

The truth was that physics formed part of her attraction to Paul. It seemed to have answers, if puzzling ones, to questions she found hard to articulate. Fan had always felt as if she were part of a world other people seemed unerringly tuned into, but that she herself perceived dimly. She felt like one of the mice Paul once told her about, who had human brain cells injected into their brains and grew neural nets rich with human cells, Frankenstein mice called *chimeras*. "They do seem smarter after," Paul said noncommittally, "for mice," but the mice stuck with her—knowing enough to consider their caged scrabbling lives with a sense of pointlessness, she guessed, but at the same time, knowing too little to make sense of it. Condemned just to watch.

Now she read her physics obsessively, her favorite magazines, *New Scientist* and *Physics World*. What intrigued her mostly involved quanta, bits like electrons that don't seem to exist in any specific space or state, strangely, until they're measured. They're in superposition, a word she loved, which meant they're blurs of possibilities, both waves and particles at once. Outside of any understandable time. Possibly entangled, so that changes in one entangled particle would cause an instantaneous but opposite change in the other, no matter how far apart. Quantum particles make up all atoms, so they're what humans are at the deepest level, but they exist according to a different set of rules. The science spoke to Fan, as her voice spoke to her spouse, in a way she couldn't put her quantum finger on.

"I want to be everything at once," she told Paul, and he replied, borrowing her unreadable tone,

"You can't. You're too complicated."

Fan realized, when she put her hand to her head, that her hair had been scraped into a bun. It was one of those perfectly round buns Korean women seemed to do with a flick of the wrist. She had felt the pull but had no idea the woman, middle-aged and standing before her in a black bikini that could have been a bathing suit but was probably underwear, edged with a little lace, had accomplished in a second this perfect globe of hair. Fan patted it in delight, like a child.

Fan lay naked on a narrow plastic table. The woman in the bikini pulled Fan's hand off her hair and placed it at her side, not gently. She had the exact look, Fan thought, of an old aunt eyeing a messy little girl, an aunt who didn't know you or care about you but somehow got stuck getting you ready for an event like a wedding.

The woman was a *ddemiri*, a masseuse whose job was to take salt and a special cloth and scrub the dead skin off Fan's body. Then the woman would massage her. Fan had not meant to sign up for a massage but the ddemiri said "Massage!" in a half shout, pointing to the word *massage* on a list of services, and there seemed no way to contradict her. None of the four ddemiri working away on nude women, all of them Korean, spoke to their clients, or smiled. When they wanted to move the women onto their backs or sides, they grabbed their limbs and flopped them.

Fan had been soaking in a warm mugwort pool waiting for her masseuse to finish with a previous client. She watched the ddemiri pound the women's bodies with their forearms; they cupped their hands and smacked the flesh, mostly around the butt, with a cracking sound like a bone breaking.

Fan, for the first time since arriving in Korea, felt anxiety welling up into her stomach. She cast her eyes around for an exit. But that was impossible; she had no clothes on, only a dim idea of how to find the locker that held her clothes, and the masseuse leveled her vexed gaze at her every few seconds. The woman had cropped hair and a physique that offered the bikini little contour.

The masseuses, most between fifty and sixty years old, had the same look, stern and unbending, as if they couldn't stop totting up the vast capacity for error found in human flesh. Yoon was right. Fan had come to the jjimjilbang, the bathhouse, only after Yoon warned her it would not be like an American spa.

The women are not "friendly like your American massage people," Yoon said, but "very professional, very trained." Fan understood this to mean they didn't flatter you, or introduce themselves, or offer you cups of cucumber water. Or rhapsodize about your fingers. Yoon had visited the U.S., and she knew.

"In your country they want to make you feel special," she said, "here it is just the body."

The jjimjilbang was indeed like no spa in the United States—cheap, utilitarian, full of families with little kids and grandmas, and with several sex-segregated floors where nude women strolled from tub to tub or dropped to stretch or do calisthenics. Fan had spent two weeks reveling in her silence and solitude before she started doing things, but even then was choosy. She joined a Korean class that met twice a week at the university, and she visited this spa. Called Dragon Hill, the place was enormous—floor after floor including pools for swimming, enormous tubs for soaking, a video arcade, places to eat, and lord knows what else.

With Fan's arm in the right place the ddemiri began working on her body. She leaned into her, using the towel and the salt and rubbing the dead skin off her in shreds and long grey rolls, curled and insubstantial as spider webbing. What was dead on Fan stripped away, literally. The ddemiri put Fan on her side and scissored her legs, she pushed her on her back, on her stomach. She scrubbed down Fan's breasts and her butt and in front stopped only at her pubic hair. Every inch of Fan gave up its dead cells, grey, thin, scattering around her as if she burned in an impossible slow burn and threw off ash. The word *dde* kept rolling through Fan's mind: *dde, ded, dead*. How strange, Fan thought, that words keep circling to the same thing, like water swirling in a drain. She imagined *ddemiri* somehow meant *death watcher*, a possible reading of the roots of the word in English, though of course it wasn't English.

At some points—at Fan's breasts, at her feet—the ddemiri's scrubbing hurt so much Fan cried out, but the masseuse did not slow down, or even appear to notice.

Every few moments the ddemiri took a bowl of warm water and poured it all over Fan's body. Now and then she poured it carefully over Fan's forehead. The ash spilled away with the water and then the woman worked the towel once more and the flecks re-accumulated.

As the ddemiri worked—leaning all her strength, her self, into the deadness at Fan's surface—she reached up to Fan's face, every minute or so, and smoothed the hair back from her temple. Like the gesture she used to form the bun, this one was quick and sure. She placed her palm on Fan's hair, sleeked it back. Fan's hair sat tight in her bun with no stray strands; her hair got wet regardless, warm water from the bowls sloshing across the table.

The gesture felt like a mother's, a pointless and absent-minded keeping neat. The ddemiri kept up the smoothing as she finished the scrub and began to massage, cupping her hands and beating Fan's ass with the bone-crunching sound she'd heard earlier. It hurt a little but not as much as the sound had promised, then made her feel alive. The ddemiri worked on Fan's feet, her back, her neck. The woman's hand, all muscle, felt light only as it smoothed down her forehead.

Fan began crying to herself, on and off, the water still draining from her face concealing the tears. At the end of the massage the ddemiri pulled the band out with one hand, grasped Fan's hair and washed it, massaging her scalp. There had been no purpose, then, to keeping her hair slicked down and wet, out of the way of the oils, the salts, the skin.

Fan cried a little more. It felt pure, to get all this woman's attention and also its complete absence. To be so wholly cared for by someone who didn't love her.

Finally, the masseuse slapped her butt with an air of finality and stepped back. Fan stood up, naked and spilling water, muscles separately jumping to life. The ddemiri punched her services into Fan's bracelet, given to her on check-in. All payment at the jjimjilbang happened on departure.

"Can I have your name?" Fan asked her.

"Uh?" The ddemiri looked startled, then waved her hand. "No, no."

Fan wasn't sure if the ddemiri had understood her and somehow rejected the idea of sharing her name, or if she had not understood. But you couldn't choose your ddemiri by name anyway. If Fan came back at the same time, she reasoned, the woman would be here. Came back when? Tomorrow?

Tomorrow might seem desperate. Fan would come back once a week, she decided. And she'd sit stubbornly in her mugwort pool until this particular ddemiri was free. Once a week—one day in seven. One was a decorous number.

Fan got back to her apartment, by cab, at around five o'clock. Paul was not there yet, but she expected him soon. He had been coming home much earlier than he would have in the States, throwing himself down on the couch with an unhappy look. He did this tonight. He had a habit when things bothered him of staring down at his thumbs, jerking them up and down, as if thinking through their opposability.

He had begun using a gel in his straight dark hair, slicking it back as Korean professional men did. Fan had always found his looks a bit generic, a little bit like the actor Seth Rogen, maybe, but cleaned up. He trimmed his beard close here and with the gelled hair looked more individual, a heavy-cheeked man with a nose that flared, and brows that never really ended, but ran across the top of his face in swards and strands.

"I don't know how to contribute," Paul said. "I don't know what they're doing. I never hear from In-Su."

"Can't you just stop into the lab? Talk to them?"

Paul shrugged and looked at his thumbs. "In-Su won't tell me the schedule. I stop in but there're just the grad students and I have to ask them what they're doing. It's embarrassing."

She wondered if he wanted her to say, *We can go home.*

She said instead: "Let's get dumplings."

Fan suggested they go to a North Korean dumpling restaurant they knew of in Insadong, a pedestrian neighborhood, then take a walk. Paul found a lot of Korean food too spicy, though Fan loved it. North Korean food was mild. Today had been a cool, sunny day. Her body, suffused with new blood and scrubbed bare, felt alive beneath her, and she wanted to walk, to move.

"Three objects can be entangled," she told Paul. "They've proven it." This news had just been reported in *Physics World*. Fan had lately become obsessed with entanglement, how human it felt in some way—particles causing one another to change but stay opposite, like a particle with up spin creating down spin in the other. Three particles entangled would also keep changing one another's states. It was bizarre and Einstein dismissed entanglement as *spooky action at a distance,* but it kept proving true. In the past, only two particles were found to be entangled.

"Huh," said Paul, idly looking at three fingers. "I wouldn't have expected that. Two makes a weird sort of sense. Symmetry or something."

"Lee Smolin thinks all particles have views on the universe. Based on their events. Perspectives. Entanglement is shared perspectives."

Fan and Paul had passed through the crowded streets of Insadong proper and moved onto a broad avenue.

"Gazillions of quantum particles in the body. Who knows how many of them are entangled. Maybe that's the reason you meet someone and you just have to see them again."

"That's poetry," said Paul.

"But particles in human bodies are entangled with particles in other human bodies. We know that."

"It's still poetry." Calling things *poetry* was not a compliment.

In bed that night Fan reached over to Paul and wedged one hand under his waist and used the other to pull his hips to her. It wasn't like her to initiate sex so straightforwardly, but her body felt too delicious to keep to herself: as soft as the tip of a petal—she couldn't stop feeling her own arms—the alive, blood-rushed surface.

Paul sank onto her, kissing her. She wondered if he would be too dejected about work to want to make love to her, but he became hard right away and ran his tongue through her mouth as if he'd lost something in there. He lubricated even before she touched him.

She placed his right hand on her thigh.

"It feels like embryo skin," he said. "What did you say they scrubbed you with?"

"Salt."

"Salt." Paul put his tongue to her shoulder. "I don't taste anything. Just you."

Funny to think she had a flavor, like an herb he might recognize in a dish.

"They wash it off."

Just the flick of his forefinger around her clit for a few minutes brought her to climax. Everything down there felt sweet and warm and full. They had intercourse with Paul on top—his choice, she was finished—and her legs wound round his shoulders. Before Paul would enter her, he asked her twice if she was sure she'd put in her diaphragm. He often did this. She wondered what had come first in Paul, the interest in cloning, or the fear of birth.

Whatever Paul might be dealing with at the lab, Fan would never agree to leave. It surprised her how much she had fallen in love with Korea, as much as it would have surprised her to fall in love with a man other than Paul. In fact, she fell in love, with Seoul in particular, the way people fall in love with other people: a visceral, even hormonal, giddy love, deep down in her body. She and Paul visited the city in the fall of the year before the move, maple leaves colored and swirling through the air like rose petals, Seoul calm and shut down for a harvest holiday.

Then the holiday ended and people thronged the streets as if they'd been poured up from the center of the earth, shopping, eating. They stayed then in Insadong. Vendors lined the streets, selling cheap clothes with delicate touches like openwork on the sleeves, dozens of kinds of foods: lollipops of scorched sugar, edible horns of soft ice cream, nuts, fruits. Yesterday's dumpling stand became today's pancakes bristling with scallion. She could hardly take it in. She reached an equilibrium she'd never felt before, so much to see and describe to herself her inner voice couldn't go beyond description and have reactions beyond an open receptive joy.

Everyone smiled at her and said what they could in English, even if it were just *OK* or *hello*, and they seemed both happy to see her and unable to see the person talking made her, whom they couldn't access. She had that feeling of teenage infatuation: as if someone has carbonated your blood.

The red of the maples was even a bit richer than a rose. She and Paul walked along a river at the edge of Insadong, a paved walkway by a channel of water. Paul saw her admiring the trees and picked up a handful of leaves, handing her a bunch by the stem. They crossed the street and he bought her a bag of walnut-shaped candy, dough molded around a nut and sweet bean paste.

"Paul! Candy and flowers!" she said, and she saw herself suddenly through his eyes: she was never so uncomplicatedly happy. He smiled, and looked nervous at the same time, rattled with wonder. She had used his name.

Fan was unsure how Paul had met In-Su (at a conference, had Paul said?), or why he'd been invited to take part in this work, given that most of his research was in agriculture. Any way of phrasing the question to him seemed to question his skills, however, and their relationship had always had that certain delicacy in regard to their work.

Paul never used the word *adjunct*. Rarely did anyone in her life: her father had no idea what it meant. He called his daughter "Professor" and could break down in tears talking about how far she'd gotten in life, *all on her own, I couldn't help her,* he'd say. Her mother had Alzheimer's; that stress and age had made him maudlin.

She would touch his shoulder. "You help me every day, Pop." And she meant what she said, though not quite in the meaning he took: his strong but bent body, knobby with old breaks, his hands dark even years removed from the machine grease and black oils of his job, reminded her she could be doing worse things than what she was doing. It was more complicated than that he had been impoverished by his lack of education, while she had been near-impoverished by its access.

Grease-monkey hands, he said of himself. And she was proud of his pride. But when she saw the course of her life, she saw a Ferris wheel that had peaked when she got her BA. She perched at the top of things staring off into the educational future, seeing a vision like a tourist brochure of a beach, a paradise—a job that couldn't be taken away from her because of tenure and that paid well, and gave her summers off. But the wheel kept turning and landed her in the same place she'd begun. She x'ed up papers instead of bathroom mirrors (with Windex; spraying in an x shape gave you the best clean); each month she paid money she didn't have to companies she didn't recognize that had bought her loans. Before her marriage she taught a full course load in the summer to keep up. All for the privilege of having a job for which she did not have to wear knee pads.

And she missed the society of her old job. Among the chambermaids, as the hotel where she worked called its maids, the position gave the women workers an equality; her smoke breaks with the other women, the times they stood rinsing out their mops together, seemed like some of the purest moments of communion she'd ever known. They had many religions and origins and ethnicities but ultimately, they were maids, the ones who put sponge and Mr. Clean Magic Eraser to the grime left by others, those other people with no sense and no shame. They laughed about the guests: who had a quickie in the afternoon; what love affairs they'd interrupted, sometimes the chambermaids in their maid outfits surprising women—now and then a man—in their own versions of maid's outfits.

This surprising of maid-dressers—sometimes just a glance through a door left a little open—happened often enough that they had a code for it: *We got company*, they said, or *We got company in 432*. Ultimately the maids as a group approved of guests for their lovemaking. They watched these guests in the hallways, reported back on their public demeanors, stacked against their private ones.

Once a week or so Fan and Yoon met to shop or have lunch. Yoon and In-Su had two little boys—five and seven, adorable—but like many Seoul-ites they had household help. She called Fan, saying simply *You want lunch? You want to shop?* either picking Fan up or telling her where to meet. For lunch Yoon nearly always insisted on a Paris Café, one of a chain of patisseries in Seoul, and Fan could never decide if this was because Yoon felt Fan would be more comfortable with European food, or if Yoon loved the chance to eat the rich pastries—chocolate tarts, Napoleons, tiramisus: she picked them up with silver tongs and heaped them on her tray. Over time Fan suspected the latter; Yoon chose her sweets while giving Fan a bright and secret smile. Fan could imagine In-Su looking down on Yoon for her love of fat and chocolate and sugar, a man who thought so necessarily about women as devices that made babies, and the stuff of babies.

Yoon tended to linger on her consonants and she had a particular and lovely way of saying the letter s, with almost a *sh* sound. When she and Yoon talked, Yoon often looked at her and let out a slow *yessss*, eyes meeting hers, a word that felt full of thought and empathy.

In their first physics conversation, Paul talked to Fan about observation. They were driving, dating. Paul wheeled this way and that to avoid bicyclists, she pretended the white line was a food the car was eating.

"It's weird," Paul said, "but it seems like until quantum things are observed they're in every possible state at once. Outside of any physical place or physical time." He told her one of the proofs of this came from an experiment known as the double-slit. In it, quantum bits like photons get shot through parallel slits. The photons remain in superposition until they hit a detector. Then the wave-function collapses and they become particles only. They're not in any definite state until they're measured.

"It makes no sense," Paul said, "but there it is. The results have been replicated thousands of times with all kinds of projectiles and quantum particles. Grad students can do the double slit. It's that clear."

"What's happening, then, when we're not measuring?"

"We'll never know. Physicists say it's like looking in the refrigerator to see if the light is on when the door's closed."

"But we kind of do know what the fridge light's doing."

"There's that."

Fan looked over at Paul, neutral as usual, jittering the wheel with one hand on top of it, one in his lap. "Why are you all there, then," she asked, "stable like that in your body? Why am I? I want to be a wave. I want to hit at things in a big messy way and be everywhere."

"Your body is complicated. And warm. Quantum effects are stronger at low temperatures." Paul's spare hand stroked his chin, as if confirming its warmth.

"You wouldn't think so."

"But within you your quanta must be all kinds of coherent."

Fan loved the language of physics: how objects in a definite state were said to be *decoherent*, rather than the opposite. *Coherent* meant in superposition, everywhere and in multiple states at once. And to be a thing like herself was to be a *classical object*. Classical objects were complex and mostly decoherent structures. But inside them, as Paul said, the little bits could pop around all over the place.

Paul said, "There are physicists like Andrei Linde who think we humans were made to detect things and keep this happening. Decohering and cohering. We participate in making the universe."

"Why would that have to happen though." Fan tapped her foot on the dashboard for a minute. She was a squirrely passenger. "Why can't what made us to watch do the watching? That sounds awfully theological."

"Linde doesn't believe in God. It's like the universe's need. Just part of the needs of existence, I guess. The rules."

"The needs of existence." Both Fan and Paul had been raised Catholic and rejected it. "Existence should have no needs."

Paul added, "Maybe the answer is we're always observed, so we're always in a definite state."

And Fan thought of Cate Crawley, a woman she watched on TV. It seemed quite true that if Fan or someone did not watch Cate, Cate wouldn't exist.

"Observation," said Paul. "It's a thing, in physics."

"Observation as reality, huh," she responded, and answered him, as she often did, with Shakespeare. "There needs no ghost, my lord, come from the grave to tell us this."

Fan thought of Instagram, Snapchat, many apps her students mentioned that she'd never heard of, like Tea and GibGab and Yakking: didn't they believe to be seen is to be real? Though the average person wouldn't know about the double slit, Fan thought, that did not mean their instincts had no merit. Popular culture offered its own intuitive cosmology.

Fan felt about Cate's show, *Crawleys Coming On*, the way she felt about physics. There seemed to be something fundamental in the world that the Crawleys, especially Cate, had figured out. As Fan watched the show, she started imagining herself in the scenes, giving Cate advice, asking her questions. In her head she talked like Cate: *Paul, you're being ridick!*

she thought. Or to Cate: *I need your thoughts on this, Cate,* she would think, although she'd also interject her own ideas into the show. *You can't live your life for your mother, Cate.*

They became one another's voices of reason.

Paul and Fan invented drinks for one another. Their drinks became little guessing games, and in Korea, the drinks came to represent physicists. One invented; the other had to guess. One would mention drinks in the morning, and it generally suggested an evening in which they'd have sex. One night, Fan came home from the jjimjilbang and met Paul, as she'd promised, at six in the kitchen. He handed her a highball glass, empty.

"It's the Heisenberg," he told her.

"And I presume my drink is uncertainty-principled elsewhere."

"Exactly." And Paul produced a bottle of Brunello, a wine she loved.

When it was Fan's turn to create a drink, she handed Paul a martini, running a spoon fast around the glass, so the gin and vermouth mixture in his hand still stirred around the olive. It quaked a little.

"The Einstein," she told him.

Paul looked at the glass for a minute. "Ah. Mass and energy. I get it."

Then Paul glanced admiration at her, which she took to mean she'd shown more imagination than he thought she had.

The week after this, after a late Korean class, Fan came home to find in the kitchen a line of plastic cups coiling around the table, each with a sip, maybe a teaspoon, of pastel liquid glazing the bottom.

"Drink," said Paul, "and guess."

She walked around the table, dripping the liquid on her tongue. It was vodka, a little sweetened, with a vaguely floral note. Ten cups' worth barely left a flavor. All the cups had a slightly different color, shading from pale violet to a series of yellows. Paul began to drink too, starting at the other end, drinking towards her.

"This would be the Hugh Everett," she said finally. Hugh Everett believed in infinite universes—the multiverse theory—and that we constantly pop out new versions of ourselves. Any multiverse theory holds that any possible reality must be, somewhere, true.

"It would be."

"You know Bryce DeWitt once told Everett, 'I like your math, but I have the gut feeling I'm not constantly splitting into parallel versions of myself.' And Everett said, 'Do you feel like you're orbiting the Sun at thirty kilometers per second?'"

"Touché."

There were days when Paul said, "I love you," and Fan spun him by the shoulder and said, "But are you splitting into parallel versions of yourself?" trying to sound jokey, and he looked at her sadly. What did he say? *Don't use science against me.*

Holding a violet drink, Fan said, "But you can't ever stop. Every second there's a choice. You'll have to walk in front of me pouring Hugh Everetts for the rest of our lives."

"What a future." Paul put his hand on Fan's ass, lightly, as if her ass were a vulnerable infant.

Fan moved away from the hand and tipped her finger into the next cup, bluish. She stuck the tip in her mouth and licked it. The lack of clear flavor bugged her.

"What's in this?"

"Vodka and simple syrup. I got a few little bottles of liqueur, chartreuse and amaretto, and I meant to get more, making each one taste different. But then I got lazy and just used food coloring."

"So this is a universe and this is a universe and this is a universe." Fan kept dipping her finger into the cups. "And the difference is food coloring."

Later that night Fan turned to Paul and said, "Victor, we live in chartreuse." Paul had no idea what she was talking about.

"The chartreuse universe. The first one we drank. For us at least. There may be in infinity of Fans and Pauls before us and after us. But we're here."

"Or we phase into another universe with each choice and just don't know it."

"It's weird to think that each of your embryos is a choice you make. You choose to clone. You choose to stick that DNA into those nuclei. So maybe in some universe they'll grow up." She glanced over at Paul, who began his unhappy surveying of his thumbs.

He said, "Terrifying," and she answered, "You knew they could be women."

Ef: Theft

Ef found she had to shove four cotton balls into the toe of each shoe to keep them in sync with her feet, rather than trying to flap off. She unwrapped the cotton balls from the little bags on her cart, slips of plastic labeled "Toiletries for the Lady," each containing two cotton balls, a cotton swab, and a tiny emery board. She had put her own shoes, brown loafers, on the bottom rack of her cart where she kept her street clothing. For her job she had had to purchase a gray uniform with a white apron sewn onto the cloth under the double-breasted bodice, for $55. This felt maybe more absurd than anything, that for a job that was all handling dirt she had to dress so particularly. All day she had to wipe at the uniform with wet cloths, to keep stains from showing. The fabric dried right away, and soon some other stain appeared.

And she knew from what happened after a change of clothes that while she wore it, she melted into her uniform; no one saw her, just it. It absorbed her. She wore the scratchy uniform until the end of her workday.

With the new shoes on, Ef walked experimentally around the room. Even four cotton balls barely kept the taupe leather shoes under control. She was a petite woman, fine-boned, with size five-and-a-half feet, six if the shoes ran small. So she unwrapped more cotton and wedged in a few more wads, adding theft to theft; the woman in this room, whom she'd run into a few times, obviously had not meant to leave these shoes here—she found one under the bed and one on its side by the tub—and her job required her to turn them in. And she was not permitted to steal toiletries from her cleaning cart; in fact, her cleanser and her cloths were monitored. Her supervisor even counted the toothbrushes she gave Ef to use for scrubbing the faucets and the grout on the tile floor.

Ef: Theft

But the shoes gave her the long, slim, tapered feet she longed for: celebrity feet, she thought. She couldn't wear heels, but even without heels, these shoes had the kind of slim elegance she associated with women like Angelina Jolie or Cate Crawley. The guest in this room hadn't thought enough about them to remember them; how could she think to get them back? The woman had kept a bag of seeds on the dresser: sunflower and pumpkin. She had a wide mouth that always seemed ready to twitch into a smile and wore the standard outfit of professional women in this town, a shapeless suit with a sweater under it.

Ef always noticed jackets and sweaters. Her mother had moved here from Naples, Italy, her father from San Juan, Puerto Rico: they had moved here and gone on to be cold for the rest of their lives. They shivered. It seemed cruel to be given a life like that, having to feel the air around you always and in such a personal way, a sting.

Ef began to clean in her uniform and the new shoes, but the backs of the shoes arched far up from her heels when she knelt on her kneepads. And the light leather seemed as if it could draw a stain easily. She changed back into her loafers, dreaming of quitting time and reacquiring her new long feet, the kind of feet that stalked across the screen in the movies or on television, toward a lover maybe, each step planted like a challenge or a promise. She could imagine herself, dressed in these shoes, being watched: purposeful, noteworthy.

Ef brought nice clothing to work with her and changed for the day at 5:30 in the maid's closet on the eighth floor, the last floor on her daily rounds, taking the elevator down as if she were a guest. Most maids went home in their uniforms, but this moment (unwinding in the chamber of the elevator and blending with guests, not one of whom ever showed a flicker of recognition that she was the woman who waited patiently at their doors while they finished Facebook posts and cell calls so she could clean) had become a ritual. It first happened when she rushed from work to get to a high school friend's wedding, then became a passage she needed to end her day, going home to where she still lived with her parents, most of her low income gone to pay them rent, the rest saved for what, she didn't know. In the moving square of the elevator, she felt the possibility of another life.

She had two dresses she'd bought from the Crawley line at Baums Department Store—a line of clothes advertised by—designed by if you believed their press—the Crawley sisters of the reality show *Crawleys Coming On*. Ef watched the show but not regularly, snapping it on while she cleaned, on various channels, so she might watch old shows, or new ones. What struck her after a while was the sense of the show as having just one timeline, one that cycled back, repeating and repeating: she would often assume episodes fit into the arc she'd just been watching, when in fact the events took place years apart: the same cheating accusations, tears, interspersed with trying on designer dresses that could look like ball gowns or science fiction battle gear. The sisters forking salads. Cell phone calls, photo shoots in which the women were filmed posing for the camera in the midst of already posing for cameras.

One of her two Crawley dresses was a tight red dress advertised as "body contouring," meaning it squeezed her body in as a girdle would. It was meant, the label said, to nudge out her curves, and it did squeeze her slim body into rolling hills where just plains had been before, out front and along the sides. The other dress was a black one with a plastic belt tooled to look like leather, a belt that tended to pierce her skin. Ef brought both with her to work and chose one to put on at the end of day, unfolding her black hair from the messy cleaning ponytail. She found that when she wore these dresses with the new shoes, though, they changed: the feel of the fabric in her hand, thin and slithery, became cheap; she noticed what she could only think of as the over-simplicity of the red color, the one-note-ness of it, and it began to dawn on her that when people found something like a dress classy, it was due to the dress being complicated, in color and in fabric, in a way she hadn't understood before.

She also realized that while the dresses did look a little like dresses the sisters and mother wore on *Crawleys Coming On*, they were simplified, dumbed down, as if the sisters tried to caricature their own style for someone they felt would never get the joke.

The camera followed the many couples on the show, from Cassie the mother and her latest squeeze, to Cate and J-lord, to the other sisters Candy and Carlotta with their boyfriends, up to the first moments of sex. It might be a scene of kissing and foreplay in bed, or maybe argument and giving in—as when Carlotta got pregnant by a boyfriend and refused sex for a while because she thought it would hurt the baby. The cameras would even stay long enough to blur the women's nude parts, though the men's never appeared. So all the Crawleys lived in a home in which each family member learned, not long after, when all of the others had had sex: the daughters had this knowledge of their mother, the mother, of her daughters. They knew whether the person wanted to or didn't really, and even whether it had been good (the cameras often swooped back in as one person rolled off the top of the other).

Did the women want to have sex, or want to have it with the men in the show rather than someone else? When Ef saw them in bed she couldn't stop wondering about this. Whose desires were expressed in those heaving bodies? Their own, or their director's? Ef imagined the family having meetings with their director about their ratings and being told which of them should have more sex, and which less. They would accept these directions with a nod of understanding and go to work.

"You, Cate," he might say. "Let's see how close we can get to a boob shot without a nipple slip." And Cate might tell J later to bend his thumb just over her nipple.

"From you, Cassie, not so much," she imagined the director adding. Or, "we'll just take the cameras out of your bedroom, thanks."

And would that ever feel like rejection? Or just like television?

It seemed odd to Ef that people valued things like clothes more because they couldn't quite pin them down; Ef felt more drawn to what she could name straight off. Though looking at these shoes—what would you call them? Was taupe right, or sand?—she felt an appreciation of such not-this-or-that-ness.

Ef no longer liked what she had. It made her nervous to steal all those cotton balls and the shoes. She kept imagining the woman who'd left them, chewing her seeds and calling the main desk to ask why her shoes hadn't been returned. The woman had stayed at the hotel in the past, she knew, and was a guest of the Trin Group, one of their big corporate clients. If anyone found out she had taken the shoes, she might be fired. And her job at the Mariposa was a huge step up from her last job, cleaning at the Sheraton, all she could find to do after a year in community college that cost too much and bored her.

On the other hand, her unhappiness with her clothing—and her desire to keep up with her feet—became overwhelming. A few days after she took the shoes, she cleaned a filthy room: used tampons dropped on the bathroom floor, bloody and rank. As she grew angry over the mess Ef noticed a blouse hanging from the towel rack. It caught her eye, the sheen of the fabric that looked soft as human skin, the complexity of the color shading from cream to camel in the folds. The buttons, little fabric-wrapped pearls. Having touched the blouse's animal softness, it became impossible that it not be hers. It matched her shoes.

You would think—Ef would have thought—that the threat of the loss of her job would, if not keep her from stealing altogether, at least keep her from wearing what she stole at work. But in fact, when she changed at the end of the day now, she wore the blouse, the shoes, and then the skirt and scarf that inevitably followed the blouse and shoes, from another guest's room, a reasonably neat one at that. Then she waited for the elevator with other guests, most heading down to dinner.

Ef realized how risky this was, the stealing, and then wearing stolen goods at work. But the person she became in these clothes of hers could only exist at the hotel, a woman who came to be in transit, riding between one fixed point and another. As guests in the elevator looked at her, she transformed, became the person she was before only in her imagination. There she could tell her fine-boned body read to others as a body well-exercised, her dark skin as tan and leisured, like Cate Crawley, a short woman who darkened her dark skin even more with spray tans. Without makeup, in a maid's uniform and a ponytail, even the Cate Crawley who existed now—the post-plastic surgery Cate—would come across much as Ef herself did at work. To be alive in the right way required others, and their looking, which handed back to you the story you wanted to tell.

Ef thought of a phrase she ran across in a book left behind by a guest, folded open on the night table: a *fleeting-improvised man*. A memoir by a man named Paul Schreber. Well, she was a fleeting-improvised woman.

Ef began to feel the shoes send out a certain energy towards her, from her cart, as she cleaned. Once in a rush—she had spent far too much time in a room, absorbed in television—she knocked them over with her bucket. Nothing happened to the shoes, but the thought of them upended made her dizzy, till she could stoop down and straighten them.

The shoes reminded her of something she'd believed as a child—that her things had feelings only she could understand. At night her mother brushed Ef's long hair, then tossed the brush into a drawer in the bathroom. As her mother drew the covers around her Ef would feel with intensity the brush's feelings—cast sideways, coughing, choking on Ef's hair. Ef would have to climb out of bed, remove the hair from the brush and place it carefully back, straight, with bristles pointing upward. Ef's mother watched her do this—Ef would tell her mother what she was doing, if her mother asked—then she went into the living room and whispered to Ef's father.

Ef did not believe as a child that there could be things that had no feelings. Nor was she certain of that now.

At the end of each workday Ef put her outfit on, feeling the inevitable end of this game of playing dress-up, yet smoothing her blouse down into the skirt with a sense of reprieve and release.

One day she stood at the eighth-floor elevator at the end of the day, slightly behind a guest, a man with short hair the color of a pat of butter. The elevators were old and ceremonious in this hotel, announcing their coming with a sound like a rushing of wings.

The doors opened and a waiter half-fell out. Another waiter stood behind him and both were laughing, clowning around. The man with the butter-colored hair stepped back, hard, to avoid colliding with the waiter, and his foot hit the toe of her right shoe with an audible crunch of leather, a sound like a hard crust breaking. He only crushed the cotton balls, but it knocked her off balance and she fell forward, pitching over as he grabbed and held her.

"Oh my God," he said, "Oh my God." He looked at her shoe, noticeably dented, at her body wobbling in his arms. "You've broken something. I broke your toe." She said nothing, enjoying the fabric of his suit, soft and complex with a sheen to it, the cologne he wore, a smell almost like cucumber, but nice.

"You must be in agony." His eyes swept from her eyes to her feet. "Can I call 911?" Then he bit his lip, as if he realized calling an ambulance for a broken toe would be ridiculous. But she could see from his slipping eyes that he had no idea what to do; he felt responsible and like he should drive her to get medical care, and probably pay, but he didn't know how to say all this to the woman he saw in front of him at this moment—a smartly dressed young woman, one who could afford a room in a pricey hotel.

"I'm ok," she said, not rushing to straighten up and out of his arms. "I'm alright." She rubbed her fingers along the end of the shoe with a bit of ceremony, pressing down on the cotton balls, as if testing her feet.

"I don't think anything's *broken*. Not broken exactly." She looked up into his eyes, holding her stepped-on foot in one hand, and leaning into him still. She brought her other hand up to the scarf at her neck, a beautiful silk rectangle of red, yellow, and orange leaves.

"It hurts," the man said sympathetically. "It's *painful*."

She planted the foot on the floor, wobbling her leg back and forth as if uncertain it could hold her weight. Slowly she pulled out of his arms, favoring her left foot, hoping she was shifting her body in a believable way. She had felt nothing when he squashed the cotton balls, though her eyes and hand had instantly seized on the shoe; she thought it might have been blemished. A thought formed in her head, *I am performing*, and she had been, though she'd done it without thinking, in the way someone on a show like *Crawleys Coming On* must do.

"Are you right-handed," the man said, then, "Oh God *that's* idiotic. It's not like you'd be right-footed," and then, "I think I should stay with you until I'm sure you're fine. I'm Tom."

She extended her scarf hand, smiling weakly.

Tom said, "I was going to grab some dinner. Can I treat you to dinner here?"

In this way Ef ended up eating dinner at a table lit by a votive candle with a white napkin folded like a goose bending its neck toward her, at the hotel where she worked as a chambermaid (they used this word here, *chambermaid*), wearing clothing stolen from women who might well be in this room, all of them sipping from wine glasses that looked crystalline-ly lovely in the low light, but that she knew were cheap—about half a buck a glass, just well washed. She had a moment of panic entering the room but it went away as soon as she sat down; the low light and the man who held her by the arm, with his suit and tie happening to pick up colors in her scarf and blouse, were both a disguise and an armor. No woman who matched her man so carefully could be a thief.

She had tasted many of the restaurant's offerings picking up room service trays, a habit all the maids had. She ordered the dry-aged steak with a swiftness that she realized made her seem like a seasoned guest. Ef was impressed with how well she handled this situation; she hadn't had a boyfriend since high school and had little sense of what a date should feel like—those high school boys had seemed dropped into her world by nature, from some sort of restless social sky.

Tom told her he worked with people but didn't elaborate. Ef told him she ran a cleaning business, thinking back to her first maid's job, for a large chain company that had franchises all over. You bought one, the woman who led her group of four maids told her, giving you the right to use their name and advertising. It seemed believable.

"We both have to work with people," Tom said, buttering bread. "People don't always know what they want."

She smiled and nodded her agreement.

Tom ordered a bottle of wine, some type that he ran past her before ordering it, though the words had gone by like music, sound without content. The waiter poured her a generous glass, and Tom kept refilling it. She grew up drinking wine with dinner, her parents' habit, but she had had little to eat today and she felt very relaxed after finishing her first glass, then a little more than relaxed: swimmy. Her steak tasted delicious, very different from her mother's made with lemon and oil, and the difference between the two steaks resembled the difference between her old and her new clothing: the old dresses had a kind of beauty, but it was simple and you couldn't have said a lot about it, while she could have talked and talked about this steak, which she'd only tried before when it was cool and congealed: its tenderness, the way the coating of peppercorns had a charged flavor but little heat, the notes of sweet and cream and mustard in the sauce. The way, like good clothing, the flavors kept subtly changing.

"I like the pepper," she told Tom, but didn't want to say too much.

Tom proved to be the kind of person who always had a question he could ask, though he didn't seem to listen too much to the answers—a good thing, because Ef couldn't invent much about running a cleaning company, and stuck to responses she had heard from her team leader's supervisor: You had to clean well—I mean, remind your employees to clean well—under the bed and under the mattress (but never, she left out, mention what you found there to the wives: tissues stuck together with body fluids you didn't want to think about, used condoms—look, her supervisor said, married couples don't use condoms, the woman in a marriage gets the birth control). For whatever reason, most of their clients were straight married couples, a man and a woman. You had to clean in such a way that people might believe the woman who lived there had done it, so another girl on the crew got in trouble for folding the toilet paper into points, the way she'd been taught at a hotel.

"So I had to tell the girl, cut it out with the toilet paper!" she told Tom. "The wives are complaining. A lot of them don't even tell their husbands they hire us," Ef added. "Sometimes they say a clean house makes their husbands romantic."

Tom smiled appreciatively, though his eyes kept flicking around the room. He had a habit of not really meeting her glance but looking at her until she looked at him, then letting his eyes slip away, though not in a shifty or nervous way. It felt confident, as if he felt certain he knew enough about her, and she liked him for it.

He was a good-looking man, though in a bland way that made him hard to describe. His eyelashes were his most striking feature, long and fair as his hair, palely framing his eyes like brushy halos. "Which room at the hotel is your favorite?" Tom asked. "I love the tub in the window one." He topped off her glass. Had he bought a second bottle of wine? He might have.

"Me too," Ef answered, thinking of the shoes.

Ef, even when she wasn't lying her head off as she was now, often found people hard to talk to. They looked at her in ways she couldn't interpret, and she felt the things she was saying were making some entirely different impression than the one that formed in her mind as she pulled the words out of their separate places and squashed them together. She rehearsed what she was about to say and anticipated the reaction, but, like a bad actor or unfunny comic, rarely got the response she imagined.

Tom, however, was easy to talk to. It didn't seem as if he were that interested, just that he could absorb the words bouncing at him and lob them back easily, pleasant, neutral, like someone playing a sport so familiar he probably wasn't more than a little conscious about it. He didn't care what rooms she liked, he just wanted to keep the word-ball moving. He had no wedding ring. He was at least a dozen years older than she was, mid-thirties, an age difference that seemed proper as long as the man was the older. Why shouldn't he want to be with her again?

Tom didn't blink at spending thirty-two bucks on her steak, and he had the suit and a watch of shiny metal, some real metal that came out of the earth like that, just needing to be polished up, with many smaller wheels telling various things within the larger wheel-face of the watch.

They were easy together in a way that promised they could always be easy together, sit together at a table and do this every night.

Ef thought: this is how people develop lives that work. They have good clothes and stand at elevators at nice hotels where someone might step on their shoes and then see them for the first time, see them as a person equally worthy.

She had another thought that caused her to jolt slightly in her seat. It wasn't just okay in the moment that she had stolen, but it was right in a larger sense: of course, stealing must be the only course of action, and people who did well in life—even those who stayed solidly in place—did it by stealing what they wanted from others, who would steal it too if they got a chance. If nothing else, successful people, like the Crawleys, decided what they wanted to be and changed into it, stealing who they became from God or the fates or whatever you happened to believe created the world as it is, and kept an eye on it.

Ef thought of all her parents' stories, their sisters and brothers and friends and even a parent who died young of typhoid and cholera and pneumonia. Or the girl known as "my cousin Maria that killed herself, God bless her," in the words of her mother, who invoked Maria and then crossed herself. Life itself was theft.

Ef noticed, by dessert, which was a custard flavored with roses and topped with a crust of sugar, that Tom's inattention and looking around the room seemed purposeful in a way she hadn't realized at first. Being nervous, she hadn't noticed, but he kept glancing, trying not to let her see, at the entrance to the restaurant, as if looking out for some particular person coming in. As she absorbed this fact, another one hit her: he had mentioned, in the stream of conversation, that he lived in town. So why was he here at all, and how did he know the rooms?

Ef thought it was likely Tom had come to the hotel for an affair, and that the affair had been going on a while. He didn't want his lover to see him in the restaurant with her; he didn't want to try to explain the toe and the waiter and his feeling bad towards her. It might have been an affair with someone married, and he might even have taken his own wedding ring off for his lover's sake. He had his own used condoms stuffed in dark places where they didn't belong. It was the other thing about life and about stealing, which had just seemed so simple and clear: sometimes what you wanted to steal had been stolen already. And your own desire, though it pierced you as you looked, say, at a blouse on a rack, maybe was not enough.

Ef got up at the end of dinner and did not think about her foot, putting weight on it as usual. Tom walked her to the outside of the hotel, a well-lit circular entrance, and said goodbye.

"I'm so glad you're alright," he told her, smiling, which scrunched up his eyes and made his pale lashes that much more visible. They reminded her of the silks from an ear of corn. Shucking ears was one of her jobs around the house—her father loved fresh corn—and she thought of the cling of the silks, which she'd be wiping off her fingers and her clothes for the rest of the day. She imagined his lashes hanging onto him as they fell, fine curls caught in the watch, on the suit. "Please call me if you need anything else."

Tom ducked down, and in the process looked at Ef's shoes, and she saw them through his eyes: on her petite body, far too large for her feet.

"I'm fine," she said, hearing the stiffness in her voice. "Thank you."

The next day Ef came to work hauling, as always, her new shoes and stolen clothes, in a Shop Rite Grocery Store bag. She put her hand into the bag without thinking about it, fingering the soft fabric of the blouse, the cotton-balled fullness of the shoes, but without a faith she had had the day before. Maybe these things, with all their ties to a certain way of living, still could not bring you to that way of living, the nightly careless conversation at the dinner table. Maybe they could only get you so far and then, like a streak of dye in the hair, they'd fade. She could not remake herself: she was no Crawley.

At work Ef saw Anna, a woman who came to the Mariposa from Portugal. She ran into Anna in the maid's closet, loading up her cart with tiny bottles of soap and shampoo and skin lotion, as she loaded up hers. She had thought about the possibility of running into Tom at the hotel that day but didn't really care. She could duck easily as if getting something out of her cart, and she doubted he'd look hard enough to notice her, just see her uniform and her hair.

One of her new shoes slipped out of the Shop Rite bag onto the floor. Anna picked it up and handed it back to her.

"Beautiful," she said, adding, "a little big?"

"Oh actually," Ef admitted, "it is big. It's not really mine." It occurred to Ef the other woman may have seen the shoes before; better to tell her.

"I guess I kind of took it. That woman who stayed in the tub room? She left her shoes here, in her room. It feels like stealing, kind of." She was a bit embarrassed.

"Ha, her," said Anna. "She always leaves a pile of stuff behind. You didn't steal it. She didn't want it. This is stealing," Anna laughed as she slipped tiny shampoo bottles into her purse. "She's odd, that one, leaving piles of crap behind, all folded neat. I guess she doesn't know what suits her."

Ef had not stolen the shoes, then. And for all she knew, maybe she had not stolen the blouse, the skirt, and the leafed scarf either; the blouse had been jammed on a towel rod, for God's sake. Maybe these women were just as glad to be rid of these things, or they had so little to do with them they never noticed their absence.

A flush crept up her neck. Maybe she had instinctively reached for the clothing these women knew, in the safety and security of their lives, was inferior; clothes lacking the magic that kept the wealthy women up above her where they floated; clothes that had deflated somehow.

When Anna wheeled out of the room with her cart, Ef poured the contents of the Shop Rite bag into the white plastic Lost and Found bin in the room. She straightened out the shoes, pulling the cotton balls out of the toes and tossing them in her open yellow garbage bag. They were all she felt truly sad about, dignified shoes, giving her feet reach and purpose. She had a little money in the bank she'd been hanging on to but as she couldn't go back to her old clothes or keep these, she would go out this weekend and spend some, find herself more, at a store where all the clothes were good clothes.

She could call that high school friend who'd gotten married and restart their friendship. She had other high school friends still in town. It might even work to go out sometime, shopping or some such, with Anna. There were always things to do, weren't there? No matter what happened to people, they did things.

And she found pleasure just in being with women. She smoked with the other chambermaids from time to time, bringing Kools she lit by pressing the unlit tip to the coin of flame on another woman's cigarette, a gesture that felt so intimate it made her startle with the thought of having sex with that woman, with women. She imagined what she might do with her hands, her tongue and would touch herself, later. At these moments, laughing, smoking, she wanted to make a move, but she felt like she didn't understand how to start or to give pleasure the right way, and would make a fool of herself, in bed.

Still, the thoughts that tumbled through her head as she wheeled toward her first rooms felt old and used, images from a self she thought she'd left behind. She had a lot of life in front of her—probably a good sixty years, all of it wheeling in front of her and heavy to push. Would she always do this, or something like it? That life to come felt like a weight in her body, something she was doomed to carry but never truly give birth to, her version of being forever cold.

At the same time, each turn of the wheel of her life was final, in a way the rooms she cleaned were not; the same rooms came back, but a day would never. It was just gone. And both thoughts—the weight of *now* and the finality of its ending—were sad.

Her mother watched a television show called *Cosmos*. In it Ef learned that the universe held endless strangenesses: warped time, or backward time, or no time, astronauts chugging along without getting any older, the vast erupting from the pinprick. There was a thing called Hilbert space and we exist within it and it has infinite dimensions, though we do not. She had felt a little of that Hilbertness, she thought, during her dinner with Tom, and then her body passed back into one dimension only, that one of rags, smears, Clorox.

Ef went into her first room. It seemed a man was staying there; she noticed undershirts draped over the back of a chair, a wide brown brush with coarse bristles, aftershave the color of blue detergent in the bathroom. She began the bathroom with Rust-Out in the toilet—the old hotel pipes sent rust-blushes onto all the enamel—a putty knife and Windex on the glass shower door.

She went back to her cart, parked in the doorway, for a rag when Anna appeared, holding the shoes in her hands, the long and elegant shoes, toes pointing towards her.

"In the Lost and Found?" Anna said, then, when Ef didn't answer, "Filomena?"

Fan: Loving a Calf as Well

She sat at Vato's Tacos in Itaewon. In front of her was an enormous plate of Vatos French fries, fries smothered in kimchi, chili sauce, and cheese. All her group dug into them. Also in front of her was a margarita in a huge glass, a glass as big as some sinks she'd used in Korean toilets. Above the sink-sized drink a bottle of beer tilted, clipped to the glass by a wire and slowly pouring into it as she swilled. The beer was very yellow.

Arrayed around her was a group: Peter, Judith, and Rebecca. They were students from her Korean class. Twice a week after class they went out together, sharing the pain of the class: though they'd learned the Korean alphabet, they could not speak. The teacher put them into a conversational group that never got far beyond *what is your name?* and *I am so-and-so* and *thank you.*

Ireumi moyeyo. Kamsamnida. Repeat.

Peter liked to say, "It's the damned diphthongs."

Now, giddy with margaritas, they kept repeating it: *the damned diphthongs.*

"Damn those diphthongs! Damn them!" said Rebecca. She and Judith taught English in a business school. Both of them were Americans and young and giggly. Peter was closer to her age and also American and he did something with Korean automakers, some car consulting thing. He worked out of the United States but came to Korea for long periods of time. In his field, he told them, the professional men spoke English.

"I'd just like to be able to walk into a restaurant and order dinner without pointing," he said, when Fan asked why he took the class. She had no such desire. The silence of her stay in Korea remained precious, a luxurious space around her. Paul had asked her to take the class; if she learned the language, she could teach it to him. Secretly, she thought he wanted her to get out more, get away from her books, the shows it slipped out she watched on her laptop.

She had no drive to learn, though, but she enjoyed being a student—sitting in a classroom with no duties to lead it. She'd become a brat, actually, winking at her friends, passing notes about where to eat after. She never did her piles of daily homework; none of her group really applied themselves. When the professor asked her why she had not she said proudly, *I am a student of physics.* Or, *a Shakespearean.* Once she said, *professor dame.* He always began to say something in response but cut himself off.

She did enjoy knowing the Korean alphabet. She could read signs phonetically in her head all day, and given how many English words Korean borrowed, it was like a game, every tenth word something you recognized. Shopping for clothes she saw tables of men's shorts, tight and long the way boys here wore them, and read the sign: *beh myoo dah.* Bermudas. Mens' shorts were Bermudas here.

Yoon was beside her, holding up a boy's tee.

"Bermudas," said Fan pointing, and Yoon said, "Yes."

Like listening in to peoples' conversations and noticing a word like *computer,* or *sandwich.* A little order resolving out of the randomness, pleasantly resolving to randomness again.

Tonight the teacher had tried to teach them to hear the difference between the Korean double and single consonants: jj and j, tt and t, and so on.

"I'm sorry but I just heard a bunch of j's," said Rebecca. "Jay jay jay jay."

"We just don't have a language that cares much about the individual letter," said Fan, though only Peter seemed to understand her. "I mean English," she added, but the women only stared.

Sitting by Peter at the Korean taqueria, Fan stole glances at his hands, which she found very beautiful, just like hands in a Renaissance painting, soft and spatulate at the tip, with long elegant fingers. These were, truthfully, hand model hands. Peter had Renaissance hair, too, that nether color that wasn't quite blond or brown or red but a little of each. His face was refined, but it struck her as bland, unlike his hands. "I need to bring Paul along sometime," she told her friends. "We've got this Biblical name thing going."

In truth she had no intention of bringing Paul along. She felt close to her group, a tight situational closeness she once felt with the other maids at her hotel. Anyway, Paul now worked till nine at night or later. He was part of the lab now, still tense but in a jazzed hyped-up way, making excuses for aspects of the place that had bothered him before, like the fact that the cells they extracted and the ova they enucleated—pulling the DNA-bearing nucleus out of the egg so they could pierce it entirely with clone DNA—came from women students who worked there.

"He's taking dozens from each of them," Paul had told her earlier. "Some of them may not be able to have kids."

Now he said, "It's their choice. They want to be part of something."

"Everybody wants to be part of something," she said. "It doesn't have to be that thing. That lose all your eggs thing."

"You never wanted children," said Paul. "Maybe they don't either."

Fan said, "They're too young to know."

Paul had even begun to defend another cloner in Korea, a man his team consulted for at times, who cloned for people—many of them rich Americans—their pets who'd passed away. This cloner charged a great deal of money, tens of thousands of dollars. At first Paul had joined Fan in finding this indulgent and creepy, and now he said, "Who are they hurting anyway?"

"You mean, besides all the failed clones that die?"

Paul made a face. "There's that."

"What do those people even do?" Fan said. "Keep clippings of their dogs' and cats' cells in case they pop off one day? So they can just make another one?"

"You have five days," Paul said. "For five days after death you can harvest good cells." For some reason Fan heard it in her head as *gu' cells*.

One day Fan was binge-watching television on her laptop when she felt keenly the way she and the woman she watched shared the same warm, animal body, had likenesses, were even the same—the way she might see two robins, or two ants, as the same.

It was one of those thoughts that come out of the blue and stop you with their rightness: the woman had eyes like she did, that drew their images from this same planet. Their similar bodies, moist and muggy, and teeming with ever-smaller parts. Though there were things peculiar to her world—the yip-yip of small car horns in the street—as there were things peculiar to the woman's: the cameras, for instance, like portals delivering her to Fan. The woman, Cate, didn't know Fan, though Cate could look into the blankness of the camera and know she filled the eyes of another woman, somewhere.

Paul would enjoy this thought-—the connectedness—but she could not share it. He disliked her watching what he thought of as silly television.

But it was hard to shake the idea: how she and the woman could be connected yet not connected, superimposed, yet not quite. And in fact she read that a physicist with the edible-ish name of Fotini Markopoulou-Kalamara calls the cosmos we each inhabit, created by our perspectives, our *light cones*. Individual, infinite in depth, narrow as hell in breadth. No two quite the same. At the moment of connection she felt herself in the woman's light cone; the woman, maybe a little bit, in hers.

Cate first appeared on TV in a minor role in a show starring a school friend, a very rich debutante who had hit the plastic surgeons before Cate did. The face this friend drew from what surgery could give had a molded plastic quality: a thin-faced Barbie with wider lips. She got famous for saying *I think you rock*. She wore no underwear and had many wardrobe malfunctions: zoomed up in the tabloids, censored on her television show by a black bar at the forbidden place. Her name was Riga. Cate then had been a pretty teenager, not much more than pretty, her nose rather wide and her face bell-shaped. Her brows, and her sisters', grew thick as winter caterpillars. She had nice legs but an otherwise normal figure.

Cate was known through Riga but followed her on television with her own surgeries and her own show and caused Riga to be forgotten, except as someone who had a place in Cate's ascendency.

You are the oddest person, Paul liked to say to Fan: if you're not reading *Lear*, you're reading *People*. And it was true.

In the silence of Korea, Fan also began writing fiction in her head. It was one ongoing story with set characters but it also morphed constantly. The woman in the story could be Molly or Mary or Marilyn and the man could be Will or Wayne. She always had red hair; he always wore a baseball cap on weekends. Sometimes the two were scientists, splitting photons together and driving far off to other labs to measure the photons and their entanglement. Over the phone they cheered about the photons' always opposing spin. But a lab assistant Fan playfully named Victor stole the pair's research and cheated them of their publications. Fan didn't feel she wanted this particular plot development to happen to Will and Mary, but nevertheless, in her head, it kept happening. And for no particular reason—the photons couldn't tell—Will and Mary sometimes kept it a secret where each set up the secondary lab, to receive the entangled particle. *Guess where I am, Antarctica,* messaged Mary.

For the first few weeks Fan intended to let her stories gel and then write them down.

But, Fan realized, if she wrote her stories down, she would have to revise them, fix improbabilities in the action, explain the science, make plans to try and publish. Now events flowed through her head in various tracks and never had to settle into one. Molly and Wayne took a boat and dipped toes in the Han River, and went home filled with lust, or Wayne could read Korean and gave Molly an appraising look after reading a note from the lab assistant. Though he told her, *It's nothing, it just says things like "get some new crystals and some film."*

For a while the pair were a modern take on Macbeth and Lady Macbeth and murdered their way to the top of a car company. Marilyn plotted in her head when she went to the jjimjilbang.

These could be good stories or bad stories, or good at times and bad at times. They unspooled in her head and when something bothered her in a story, she changed it or started over. She never mentioned what she was thinking about to Paul.

She and Paul still took walks. October was as beautiful as it had been in their short visit, and then November was unusually warm. Hongdae had long, steep streets with students from all over, eating cheap food from street vendors and going in and out of the clubs and bars—Mexican, Irish, and even Texas-style bars, though all of them had anachronisms: the Texas bars always seemed to have an Elvis image out front. Young men played guitars on street corners; one sang a language Fan couldn't place. It turned out to be Bob Dylan's *Lay Lady Lay,* sung with a heavy accent, not Korean.

Paul never wanted to talk about his work these days. "It's about getting viable stem cell lines out of the blastocysts, then getting the pluripotency, you know, you can make any cell in the body out of them, and you want histocompatibility," he said in a rush when she asked how it was going. She knew, because she asked, that Paul and In-Su were starting to seed interest in a paper on their work.

"We're aiming at *Biologique*," Paul told her with that new jazzed-up nervous energy. He had published there before, and it got him his tenure.

"Blastocyst," she said, hung up on the word: *cyst* from the Greek for *pouch* or *bladder*, so a blasted one seemed not viable at all.

They paused in front of the Hello Kitty Café, a small coffee shop, thick-pink, with an enormous pink bow above the door. Fan imagined her characters going in to have a coffee and discuss their relationship, not noticing all the Hello Kitty décor until they'd been talking a while.

She peered inside: it was all the same saturated womb-pink, with a white Hello Kitty statue by the door and little ears on the napkin holders. She dropped that story line. Not very likely.

"Are you getting homesick?" Paul said. He'd been asking this lately.

"No, not really."

"I wonder how the garden's doing."

Fan shrugged. "It's established. It'll be fine."

She had noticed, in the past few weeks, two beggars on the route they liked to walk, from their apartment to Meat Street where the barbecue places smelled so charry-delicious, then down to the street with a name that translated as Likes to Walk Street. Tonight, she passed both men, begging, a block apart. One of them had no shoes. He wore rectangles of Styrofoam cut from a cooler tied to his feet with string. He clomped along like an Elizabethan woman on her pattens, high clogs meant to rise above the running sewage of the time.

The other man had a broken leg. The jag in the bone was visible and he had wrapped it around with cardboard doweling, an improvised cast. He half lay and half knelt in the street, his torso supported by a pallet. He had an American baseball cap, laid out for begging, too grimy for her to see the team name.

She saw so little poverty in Korea that when she noticed it, she found it hard not to think about. It occurred to her that these men—the one who had no shoes but slabs of Styrofoam wobbling beneath him, the one with cardboard around an injured leg that probably wouldn't get a chance to heal—valued life, clung to it, in a way that she never would, a way that formed a labor she in her life and her work and even her dying would probably never know.

Rebecca and Judith came with her one day to Dragon Hill. She had stuck to her plan of going once a week. She always waited for the ddemiri she'd had on her first visit, waving away any other masseuse.

She hated going with these women, her friends, and had tried to get out of it, but they insisted.

"It's so much more fun when you're with somebody," said Judith.

"I feel like I stick out when I'm alone," said Rebecca.

Fan ended up using a different ddemiri—she could not think of a way to explain why she'd wait for her usual masseuse. They sat in the pool together before their scrubs. Rebecca and Judith had a passing resemblance—blond hair, regular features, brown eyes—but their bodies turned out to be very different. Rebecca had breasts like sunny-side-up eggs and a handful of fluff at the crotch, with a straight waist. Judith's breasts sat high up on her ribcage, above a slender waist and broad hips. She had nipples shaped remarkably like the nipples on baby bottles, more so than any Fan had ever seen. Her dark blond pubic curls spilled down her thighs.

"I miss Peter!" said Rebecca. "Wouldn't it be weird to be hanging out here with him!"

"He's so funny. What a mimic!" echoed Judith.

Rebecca and Judith started laughing about the Hello Kitty café and Fan moved slightly away from them. She could laugh about things like the Korean class after a few margaritas but didn't like herself for it. This laughter hurt her; it felt like someone mocking physics, or something else she deeply loved, and found complicated. She suspected if these women knew more about her background, their reaction wouldn't be kind either.

"They built that Hello Kitty café thirty minutes from a country that wants to bomb them," Fan said. "I never knew before I got here that North Korea was so close to Seoul." She realized as she said it that her defense of the café probably made no sense to them: that to her the place seemed not kitschy but brave. It felt heroic, the way Cate Crawley could feel heroic: putting her imagined self out there every day for the public to mock and critique.

Peter, for all his japing, would be on her side in this judgment. They talked about Korea one day and Peter said abruptly, *I feel like I'm a good soul here.*

In any case, the women paid no attention.

"Peter'd love to see *you* nekked. You know he has a crush on you," said Rebecca to Fan.

"Yeah no kidding," said Judith, picking old glittery polish off her toes.

Fan's scrub was the first one she had that did nothing for her. She had none of the usual release and purgation. She was back to self-consciousness, making grimace-smiles at the ddemiri. Her body held on to its new sense of inertia. As the ddemiri moved away to scratch what Fan owed into her bracelet, she noticed her usual ddemiri had stepped out. In a cubby by her table her ddemiri kept her extra bikinis. Without thinking about it, Fan reached in and grabbed a bikini top, a black and practical bra edged with lace. She cupped it in her fist, then pushed it down her blouse as she dressed and walked out with her friends.

What Rebecca and Judith said was true, she realized, thinking about it at home in her apartment. She had put the bra on herself; soaked in massage oil, it smelled salty and fruity, adding to the peach tea odor of the apartment. Her chest mounded out of the little triangles the athletic masseuse filled out only slightly. Fan put her blouse back on but didn't bother buttoning it and kept fingering the bit of lace, which reminded her of the orange flavoring added to children's medicine, a bit of sweetening for the staid and useful.

Though maybe *crush* was the wrong word. Peter was in something with her—in lust? In erotic curiosity? She sensed it was not a feeling that mattered much but consumed him at the moment. When the group went out together, during their first and second and third round of drinks, he stared at her when her eyes seemed other-where, perhaps engaged across the table with Judith's or Rebecca's. His eyes bored into her as if boring into her image could itself be intercourse. She had begun flirting with him, tapping his hand to make a point, winking at him to punctuate a joke.

He claimed to be single but could easily not be.

When Paul came home that evening she still sat there on the couch, her blouse unbuttoned. Lately she had gotten out of the habit of doing anything about food. (She did not do much laundry, either, and often ran out of clean clothes and ran out to buy new underwear and a top from a street vendor.) Paul picked things up at vendors or noodle or dumpling shops on his way home, or he ate with In-Su and the lab team, and she had dinner with her class, or on other nights, just ramen or peanut butter.

Tonight he let himself in and sat next to her and handed her a paper cup filled with dumplings stuck with street vendor chopsticks, basically just long thick toothpicks.

"Thank you," he said, turning around and taking her in.

"For what?"

"Oh." The corners of his mouth pinched. "I thought you put that on because you wanted me. Wanted sex."

The bra. They hadn't had sex in a while, had they? She hadn't been thinking about it. No new drinks. So she ate her dumplings and they did, and it was nice, but she kept thinking about Mary and Will and how they might have Macbethian sex, and what would that be? Calling on spirits together? Too hokey; she couldn't make it work.

She asked Paul to do one thing with her every week, one thing of her choosing. He was always busy now. He was both obsessed with his research and unwilling to tell her much about it. He and In-Su had a draft of their paper, and it had to do with getting the stem cells to turn into brain cells, which Paul implied but didn't quite say they had done. Getting brain cells from stem cells, with all that promised for people with things like Alzheimer's, was a Grail of cloners and she wanted to be more involved in it—look in at the lab from time to time, share his pride—but Paul said that wasn't the Korean way, no wives in the lab.

"I think you're afraid In-Su will attack my eggs," she said.

"I can't guarantee the safety of unescorted ova."

There might be a bit of truth in it; Paul said their work took thousands of eggs just to get a few lines of stem cells. In her imagination the lab resembled a chicken farm, crates and crates of laying women, eggs gleaming everywhere, lolling shells cracked open.

"Lord," she said, and, "I wish you could make some brain cells for my mother."

"Having cells isn't having a treatment. That's way down the road."

She chose the Han River cruise partly to irk Paul. It was very touristic, a gaudy two-tiered ferry that went down the Han with a voice-over in English and Korean narrating the sights, and a truly awful pop band. She and he stuck out and looked unsophisticated and Paul hated that. Right now the band was blasting Katy Perry's "Teenage Dream," singing in a stiff voice that arose from singers trying to approximate a language they did not wholly know.

Fan had no real desire to be here either. She would rather have been with Peter and Rebecca and Judith. Lately the group had been getting together on days when they had no class. The evening before this the four had met to go to a restaurant at the edge of Namdaemun market and as they walked together through the outdoor stalls, she stopped and bought a bra plushed with lace—a scanty bra the color of the Hello Kitty Café—and matching bikini panties. She bought these things with Peter standing there, his slim fingers tapping against his own waist.

The sun set while she and Paul waited in line to board and found their seats on the lower tier of the ferry, light draining away faster than Fan would have thought it could. Light's wave nature seemed on display; it drained off like water. For a second as she seated herself and looked out, Fan saw the dark air and dark water reach equilibrium, then lights began to ping on and bring the buildings back, all edge and soar in the black.

Seoul had 10 million people in its metropolitan area, a megacity. The skyscraping apartment towers stepped back one after another for more miles than she could guess, all the way to a mountain fading on the horizon. Their boat passed under many bridges, some, the voice-over said, holding rubble from the Korean War, some the paths of martyrs during the Japanese Occupation. Between bridges the breadth and the width of the buildings, the offices, officetels, apartments, obliterated the world.

What if, she wondered, you turned out the light for everyone who felt his or her life was lacking, everyone who wanted to be somewhere other than here, where they lived, pushing evening away with their light? What would that night look like?

Staring into the water she thought of drowning. It could happen; she could fall in. She could even be standing on one of these bridges they passed and feel she had to jump, that way you do, so close to an edge it's irresistible. Everyone felt this pull; mustn't people do it sometimes then?

She looked at Paul. He was absorbed, his mouth set in a way that made his cheeks look fat and childlike. How could he stand losing her? It struck her: he couldn't. He could not be alone and would not again have the energy to find someone.

What would he do? Of course. She pictured the five days he'd have to scrape off her cells, get them squirming in a dish, inject them into the enucleated ovum of another woman, an egg sucked dry of its genes.

And then he would have to wait, how many years, for her to grow? At least twenty and even that would look pervy. There would be the deformed Fans—deformed Babes, ironically—bull-headed, gorged, tongued as if hung. He would have to do it, like the man who constructed a cast for himself out of dowels—a horrible substitution, but the only one possible.

He had come to love her in a way that had grown or at least changed, a love she sensed she would never herself experience or understand. This love had grown beyond her job, beyond what pieces of themselves they put inside one another, how he could tell her the way In-Su and the lab made him feel about himself. Beyond what he experienced as her beauty. This had happened here in Korea; somewhere inside the new jazzy antsy Paul things had shifted. He loved her beyond *her*, almost: the *her* of cloning jokes and boats, down to some selfhood he'd discovered that even she wouldn't recognize, and that his work taught him to find.

She touched his arm. "Hey."

"Hey."

"It's pretty. Huh?" She poked him. "Pygmalion. Come on."

"Mmmmm." He was annoyed and did not want to speak. *Oh, for fuck's sake, you'll probably like my clone better.* Fan looked back out at the city and the water. Marilyn and Wayne rode the ferry holding hands after a long day at the lab, Marilyn's auburn hair getting tangled in her mouth. They leaned together while a corona of light blazed up on the shore. A burst of fire, a hurling that came in arrow-shaped from the North and when it hit the ground, it exploded. They became Will and Mary, who realized that the present could never be trusted, that every touch could be the last, and their warmth heated each other's hands, they breathed in each other's odors, recognizing that they were present to each other in the way of things like fire and food—warmed, scented, flavored, temporary.

After the river cruise the picture kept surfacing in her head: her corpse (perhaps wet and streaming), Paul asking for a moment alone. Where would he harvest the cells? The cheek, that DNA cliché? A scrape of her arm? Under the nails—no, that was a cop show place to get DNA from a person's murderer. She recalled something Paul had told her, that the place you harvested the cells from influenced the outcome. In some species, using cells from the skin tended to cause morbid obesity, while muscle cells did not. He would have to bring a syringe or other instrument to dig down under the skin. Piercing her. It would be awful for him. But he would do it.

She met Peter alone for dinner. All the group had plans to meet up, then Rebecca and Judith were called to an evening meeting at their school. She knew seeing Peter alone was a bad idea. Yoon even texted her and, uncharacteristically, suggested dinner.
"I'm busy," she thumbed back, "thank you though," then stared at the phone in her hand as if the phone had written this.
So they found themselves, a couple, a man and a woman appraised by everyone they passed (who bothered appraising them), in the conservative military atmosphere of the Itaewon neighborhood, as a twosome. Peter guided her to the table with a hand on the back of her blouse. She had worn a low-necked purple dress, with the black bra underneath. Fan looked at the characterizing glances they got walking into Vato's Tacos, and the looks that sized them up and then glued them together gave her pleasure. She imagined some of them thought of the four they normally saw and recognized the winnowing of three women down to one.
She was saying, "It'd been Shakespeare all along."
She had just caught up on her back issues of the *New York Times*, delivered to her laptop, and gotten the news that the parts of *The Spanish Tragedy* she'd focused on for much of her dissertation—the so-called Additional Passages, long textual additions by a different author than Kyd—had actually been written by William Shakespeare. The authorship was discovered through spelling analysis. When she wrote the diss, scholars mostly attributed the writing to Ben Jonson, a theory she used. She loved those three hundred lines of theater—*It was a man, sure, that*

was hang'd up here; a youth, as I remember: I cut him down—and argued Jonson had used them to intensify the themes of doubling in the body of the play by Kyd. The grief-stricken Hieronymo, for instance, invented a double for his child, pretended the hanged man he found was someone other than his only son.

"My adviser said forget Shakespeare. But then he ended up steering me right to Shakespeare."

Peter said, "Wouldn't Shakespeare love that though. Fate."

"It's like my adviser was one of the witches in *Macbeth*. Pretending to push me away from what he was pushing me into." Peter gave a genuine laugh. Paul would not have understood. Peter majored in literature in college, or so he said—in any case, he was very well read.

They ordered their beery margaritas and some food to share. Vatos served its Korean-inflected Mexican food in huge portions. It was a sharing kind of place, though between her and Peter, this too felt intimate: choosing together what to order, recalling each other's likes and dislikes, the way Peter kept his elegant right hand lying out on the tiny table, close to his drink, true, but more than halfway across to her, as if he anticipated her hand meeting his.

What would happen? She promised herself she would not initiate anything. Though she kept her conversation carefully away from topics that would involve Paul, so as not to remind Peter he existed.

Peter worked in car marketing. He didn't write individual ads but worked on larger campaigns of consumer perception and branding.

"Who was the genius at Toyota who named a car Cressida?" she said. In Chaucer, and later in Shakespeare, Cressida was the archetype of the fallen woman.

Peter had thin lips, almost inverted looking, but expressive: he stretched them out like rubber bands when amused. "I know, right?"

"They should make it the Toyota Hooker."

"That car sold, though," said Peter. "Maybe a little subliminal advertising there. Like, it's more than a suburban four-door."

"Soccer practice by day, hot Greek warriors by night." She was already halfway through the margarita. "Maybe you should start pitching some other Shakespeare names."

"Who was the prostitute from the Falstaff plays? Doll Tearsheet?"

"The Toyota Tearsheet."

Peter was easy to talk to. He told stories of annoying car executives and she told stories of annoying students. She told him her name was actually Frances—the name Fan was a teenage pretention she'd taken on and stuck with. He had taken to calling her Frahn-*sess*, with a funny false grandiosity. My dear Frahn-*sess*.

She felt swept along an unruly water, and it would dash her where it would. She had written the dissertation she'd meant to write, though she had tried not to write it. Truly, if she'd thought about why she'd been so drawn to those three hundred-some lines added to the play, she might have discovered the Shakespearean authorship, reaped the literary glory. She could have had a job that would have held her—tenure meaning *bound*—paid her well, and resulted in invitations to teach in beautiful places, like Korea. And she would have been distinguished, well known in her field, so no Paul.

No one could control their entanglements.

Fan thought about chaos theory and Edward Lorenz's comment on a butterfly flapping its wings and causing a volcano. She told herself that this was margarita science, she'd never respected chaos theory. Though right now it had its appeal. As they drained their margaritas—mostly beer at the bottom of the glass—Peter stretched his hand out a little further.

"You know, I'm very attracted to you." He lifted one eyebrow slightly and his lips retreated even further.

Blood pounded in her ears; it pounded *this is real*.

There were things that would prick her later—he had not said *love*, well, that would have been too much. He had not said *beautiful*, though in the course of a week she would generally hear that word from at least one person about herself. He had not said anything about her, in fact, only about himself, but in the moment what crashed around in her head had to do with the thisness of it: the adrenaline burst, the racing heart and pulse in her ears, the way something she had pictured slid so neatly from her head into existence, into a pair of other eyes, watching her, brow lifted, from across the table. What was private and held within her opened.

"Same," was all she could get out.

"Well then," said Peter, "what do we do about it?"

The wall around the window was inexplicably covered in Astroturf. Maybe for people who wanted to have sex standing up, she thought, though running her hands through the false plastic grass, it did not feel very comfortable. Why not fleece? Padded silk?

The main challenge for Fan, the real mental problem, was the tub. There was a bathroom—a normal bathroom in light of the pink, faux weirdness of the room, a white bathroom, with a toilet and a shower. But the tub was not in it. Instead it lay angled between the bed and a faux window that was actually a mirror.

Why this strange marooned bathtub? Unlike the tub room at the Mariposa, this room held nothing the person in the tub could look out on. Too small for any two adults to fit in, barely room for an average-sized woman like herself. The room the same saturated pink as the Hello Kitty Café, except the tub.

A nightmare to clean, she thought to herself. Someone new in the tub practically every hour, and the tub having to be the one thing in the room that was white.

And changing and changing the sheets. She did not see any maids around but promised herself she'd leave a tip.

Sarang bangs, the kind of hotel where she met Peter, translated from Korean as *love rooms* and were hotels that rented rooms by the hour, cheaply, so they were mostly used by people to have sex. Koreans had tiny apartments and often lived with parents and grandparents, so plenty of sarang bang traffic consisted of real couples, not just trysting folks like herself. These hotels were hardly lush but not sleazy, slightly smutty in some ways—the *Knock Knock Knocking on Heaven's Door* in woodcut on the wall above the clerk who checked them in, for instance—but more innocent, in that Hello Kitty way. A cartoonish pink rotary phone. Pink swirls in the paint. *Kinderporn*, she thought. The hotel sign had its name outside in English—Hotel 2 Heaven—and under that

> Luxury Space!
> Lovable!
> Stylish!
> Color!
> Graphic Arts!
> Vintage!
> woo

The "woo" stood on its own, uncapped and unpunctuated. *Woo* could mean "jewel," or "treasure," or just "cute." Apparently being woo did not have to sell itself.

Peter turned the faucet of the bathtub on but made no move to undress.

"You," he said, and her heart dropped a beat and landed, thudding, on the other side of it. She realized he listened to himself saying this, had practiced saying this. He seemed to anticipate a room with a tub angled toward the bed. The light in the room was filtered but still fairly bright. She had no idea how to remove her clothes, how to take a bath in front of a man. She could ignore Paul in their apartment. Peter was an audience, a man looking forward to the pleasure of seeing a woman in her bath. She noticed a bar of soap in the soap dish clinging to the tub. Dove soap, used by other guests: concave, ridged. Should she wash herself? Did he, perhaps, want her to, being a man who worried about cleanliness? If so, wouldn't used soap bother him? There was a decorous way to be sexy in this situation. She didn't know what it was.

She felt a rush of anger at herself. Why hadn't she thought of this? You did not just find yourself naked in a bed in a pink room (as pink as the most intimate parts of your body), having sex. You had to get there. You had to take things off, things like black bras edged with lace, with your mole-blind fingers and your hands that only went so far.

Maybe with a Vatos margarita in her she could do this, but it was two in the afternoon. Though shouldn't he have brought some champagne? Isn't that what men did in these circumstances?

"What," she began, and couldn't complete the thought.

"You look beautiful. Why don't you warm up in the tub," said Peter. It maybe came out of him a little easily. Was that a trace of annoyance on his face?

Her dress's sweetheart neckline barely covered the black bra. It made her look busty in a way she liked, full curves spilling upward. The back of the dress was high, so her arms strained when reaching for the zipper. With Paul, if she stepped backwards toward him at a time like this, he would know to pull it down. With Peter she would have to ask. She couldn't quite do that, so she smiled and tugged at the zipper, her smile (which she tried to form as vague and seductive) freezing on her face.

In her frenzy she clawed a long scratch in her skin. She finally grasped the zipper and fumbled it down six inches, just enough to wiggle out. And the black bra, which, having been soaked in salt and water and oil every day for years, had a stiff, almost canvas quality and a buildup on the hook that made it hard to remove. She let the dress fall to her waist and, maintaining her smile that quivered with nerves but was set, she began trying to scrape the bra hook out of its little eye. Every time she thought she'd pulled it out she realized that no, the hook sat implacable.

Finally she did what she had never seen a woman do in the movies: slid her bra straps down her arm, twisted the back of the bra to the front, and picked the hook apart, Peter watching and her aware the movement probably gave her a double chin. Then she pushed down her black lace panties, bought for this meeting, and tried to step out of them gracefully, though they got caught between her toes and she had to bend over, the flesh of her stomach forming rolls though she was a slender woman.

"You scratched your back," Peter said, and she couldn't read his tone.

She thought of Henri Bergson, who wrote that comedy came from the failure of the body to perform up to the spirit's standards. But this wasn't funny; no one dropped into the room with them would find it funny. All would cringe. And she thought of a problem in philosophy, one used by Plato and Aristotle, in which philosophers argue that things, like an arrow flying from a bow, can never get to where they're going because each unit of distance can be divided in half and in half again and in half again ad infinitum so the arrow will always be some shred of distance—some unit of half—away from the target. She felt its truth. There would always be some unit of time and distance, some task she needed to do, before arriving at the bed.

"What nice tits," said Peter. He cupped his Renaissance hand with its long fingers around her right breast. "A nipple like a peach stone."

"A nipple like a pit?"

"My mother called them stones." He flicked the nipple between his forefinger and thumb. She realized another moment from her imagination had crash landed into the physical world—she had dreamed his fingers doing this very thing. Though, she saw now, in her daydreams she was not in her own body. In them she watched herself, a woman with masses of black hair and very round breasts, from a distance, maybe half a room away and a little above. The view changed from inside her flesh:

his fingers flicked at her nipple as if she was a computer and it was her tracking ball.

What had stayed coherent in her imagination—in flux, fluid, everywhere at once—had decohered here. As a classical object, the affair sunk in its own physicality.

She wondered if she should act aroused. She did not want those fingers exploring any farther so she stepped into the tub.

She thought, *Nothing*. Not the King Lear nothing but the nothing of Hamlet: *nothing* was Elizabethan slang for a woman's parts. If only she could become nothing but her nothing.

She stayed in the tub for ten minutes, which seemed like the right number of minutes to warm up and to establish herself as uninhibited and sexy, let him admire her soft tended mounds through the veil of the water. She chose to splash herself rather than wash. Then

hand me a towel, please, she said as she stood dripping.

"Beautiful." Peter handed her a towel, looked at her as he pulled back the covers of the bed. He yanked off his polo shirt and stepped out of his khaki pants and boxers and got in.

She thought while making the brief journey to the bed of all the things people had to walk themselves to do: meet with bosses knowing the meeting was to fire them, put their heads on chopping blocks or their butts in electric chairs. Become mistress of some crazed king who had noticed them in a crowd in their green beaded gown.

And she was there. She placed herself in by sitting at an angle and tucking in her legs.

Peter had brought some kind of cinnamon-scented oil. He rubbed it on her breasts and all around her pubic mound, over and over. She touched his penis—firm and smooth as scrubbed skin—and used the oil but did not look. They kissed and his lips felt dry and his tongue static, not like Paul's. He entered her with her legs held up and it stung. She was not aroused enough for sex but she wouldn't be, so she just panted companionably along with him. In her head she retreated to the jjimjilbang, her skin still damp making it easy, imagining the plastic table underneath her. She took his hand and placed it on her temple. He moved in her and after some minutes it was over.

She re-dressed more easily than she had undressed; he wasn't looking. They kissed at the door of the room and left apart.

She took the subway home and all the way her heart pounded in her ears as it had at Vatos Tacos. Everyone on the subway looked wrong—one woman's stiletto heels, a young girl's K-pop tee, a man's white shirt and thin tie. They existed in a new relationship to her. This must be what people meant by sin: an unwanted shift in appearances.

There would never again be a world in which this had not occurred. And she had forgotten to leave a tip.

In the next few weeks her free time grew, bloated. She quit going to Korean class. She did not want to see Peter again and he, who had texted her several times a day in the past, did not contact her. She could not see Rebecca and Judith either, without seeing Peter. Paul came home late and left early.

She went to the jjimjilbang and she also saw Yoon, who seemed out of sorts somehow. Yoon still ate her desserts but with an abstracted air, as if she were remembering chocolate and cream rather than sinking into them. She no longer treated Fan like a clever child when Fan spoke, or corrected her Korean, gently, when she tried to use it.

Paul too had grown abstracted. For a week or so he came home ecstatic, with peer reviews from *Biologique* on their paper: *Groundbreaking*, he read to her: *these data tell the story, it's a game changer.* He read quotes to her aloud and she watched his face, only that.

"Don't you see," he said after a while. "They really mean it. My people don't exaggerate. They don't use metaphors."

"It's not a patch of ground, or a game, so they're metaphors one way or another," she said.

"You know what I mean."

She'd likely ruined it for him; for that or whatever reason, he stopped reading her his reviews. It was winter. They'd passed the Christmas holidays in Korea, a day they had had guests over, something they'd not been doing much of. But they had an open house on Christmas and Yoon and In-Su came, with others from the lab, to eat turkey with them, which the Korean guests splashed with gravy and gochu jang chili paste and soy. In-Su used ketchup. Rebecca and Judith stopped in; Peter had flown home to the States. Then Western New Year and a month later, Lunar New Year went by, both celebrated in Seoul. Fan had lost most sense of time, until the day at the sarang bang.

The sarang bang day set the clock ticking. She watched the Crawleys and read books without much interest. And while she still loved Korea in that crush-y way, she knew at the same time she had mistreated her love; had allowed it to be *too, too sullied*. It had given her the gift of time stuck to no particular activity and of pleasure—touch, taste, pretty things to buy on the street and put on—time that she could nearly always barter easily for happiness. The gift had dissolved in the waters of the tub.

Who'd put a spell on the two people who kept her company? Both Paul and Yoon seemed always to be looking back or looking ahead, plucked out of the present—now a room on the other side of a glass, and they saw her through it. Apparently through the glass she was harder to focus on.

At times she wondered if there was any chance Paul knew what had happened with her and Peter. Unlikely; he was barely able to think about her, and seemed oblivious to her sudden distance from the Korean class, and her friends there. He never asked if she went to class, or what she'd had for dinner. If he'd guessed, she would be all he could think about.

He was half-in, half-out, in the little time he spent with her, and got further out by the day. Then one Wednesday in late February he came home early, a little after four o'clock. She lay on the couch reading the *Times* and *Entertainment Weekly* on her computer, flipping back and forth. She had happened upon two very different stories on the Crawleys. *Entertainment* interviewed Cate Crawley about her desire to act. She planned on taking a small role in a slasher film to build up her skills, and talked about practicing screaming, in the inner core of her bathroom.

The *New York Times* ran a story about who the Crawley family members would be if they'd been scripted by Shakespeare: Cassie became Lady Macbeth, Cate Cleopatra, Candy a serving wench, Carlotta Mistress Quickly from *Henry V*, and J-lord the generic Fool. Of course, women in Shakespeare's plays were played by young boys, not actual women, but maybe that fit the story, as the Crawley women's bodies worked so hard to play the role of women's bodies.

Paul crackled with that weird energy he had these days, as if his nervous system were a network of matches, striking. She could almost see his charged mind giving off light.

"Frances, you need to pack," he said, and "we're leaving," though he never ever called her by her proper name.

It was just what she needed him to say. How had he known?

PART II

Ef: This Ordinariness

F, Ef, Effie. Filomena, Fil, Filo, Meen, Mena, even Mena the Mean. Filomen, pronounced *File-low-men,* by people who had no idea what to make of her name. Meany-Girl, Meeny-Meeny-Bo-Beanie (sometimes shortened to just Bo-Beanie, and both names given to her by her mother), F-Bomb, FM Radio, by a high school boyfriend named Jeb, who had been the first boy to put his tongue in her mouth, which startled the life out of her (at first she didn't quite get that it belonged to him, and felt as if a wet slug wandered in there). Fuckwad or F-wad (said lovingly by a cousin). Celeste, the name she gave to Tom, as she had never run across a Celeste who did not seem wealthy.

Ef rarely heard her full name aloud; only her mother and father used it, and they didn't use it often. Mostly she went by Effie or just Ef (*ef* as in *theft,* she thought to herself). She had no idea how Anna knew her real name.

Ef took the shoes from Anna and pressed the soft leather with her thumb. It felt startlingly warm, almost alive still, as if the shoes had not quite separated yet from her feet.

"If you don't want them," Anna said, "take them to a resale store. They'd get some money on consignment. They're nice shoes." Anna looked at them again. "I've taken a lot of that Ellen's stuff to the store on Kauffman. Ruby's."

"Ellen's?"

"The one who left the shoes. The one who leaves stuff. Every time she stays here she introduces herself to me. She must have introduced herself to me like ten times. Then she smiles in that weird way, like she's told you a big secret." Anna picked a hair off the apron part of her uniform, holding it up to look. "White? Is this even mine? Anyway, she tips and she leaves good stuff. Ruby's will give you half what they get for them."

Ef took the shoes back and stuffed them into her cart.

It turned out to be a long day. It happened: sometimes the hotel drew into itself hundreds of hopeless people. People who used five towels in a one-person stay and left them soaked on the rug. People who could not get one thing out of a suitcase without upending it all over the floor, which would also be littered with wrappers, both candy and condom, or both (and dropped in what order, thought Ef?). One tub broken out in measles spots of pink all over the inside, and Ef couldn't decide if they were nail polish castoffs or lipstick. Either way, who pressed their wet nails or their lips to a tub? Carpets bore the outlines of shoes in pitch-like shoe polish.

The maids cracked *Saturn in retrograde* to each other, and they said, *I'd love to see his wife get after him*! of a man who left his bathroom a spatter of foam, whisker shards and thrown towels. It was a fantasy of theirs—always a husband or a wife (generally a person of the opposite sex) waited offstage, one who would later enact upon the person the maids' fury.

Ef had gotten in the habit of watching television while she cleaned. She had a half hour per room, so she made an effort to start each room right on the hour or half hour if she could, to follow her TV schedule. If she got deeply involved in a show and couldn't finish it, she'd wait till the last minute to snap it off, then half-run to the next room, snapping it on again. It was not precisely against the rules to turn on the television—many maids did it—though she did worry someone would complain about her channel settings. Mostly she watched *Crawleys Coming On* or one of a few television preachers.

Ef found that, after her dinner with Tom, she remained confused about her relationship to the hotel: *who left my room like this*, she'd wonder, entering the disorder. And at times when the TV was on she'd find herself sitting in a chair, or on the bed, to watch, as if she had all the time in the world.

Ef watched the Crawley show mostly to see how the C-Raws, the Crawley women, looked and dressed. In the course of watching she learned all of the resources the sisters and Cassie had to look perfect: Botox, boob jobs, Spanx, nose jobs, lasers, butt jobs, lipo, dye, facelifts, hair extensions, waist trainers, neck jobs, spray tans, makeup artists with palettes of color and hundreds of brushes, not to mention the swimming-pool sized closets of designer clothes. The tans fascinated Ef: the women crouched in a shower stall, nude, while from the end of a hose held by some man, darker skin bloomed. Then they became brown as her, but it was different, glowy and perfectly even, implying they could even borrow the skin of people mostly poorer than they were, but wear it wealthy.

The way the faces of the Crawley women looked, in relation to real faces, reminded Ef of the difference between a forest and geometric planes of farmland—smoothed, terraced, colored a near monotone except for the dramatic play of light and shadow. Like parts of Italy, which she'd seen with her mother. Ef felt she desperately wanted to learn things from the show, but she couldn't learn anything from all this—just that she needed far more stuff, and people, in her life than she had.

So Ef concentrated on the preachers, whom she had started watching one day on a whim. Her choices had been a minister named Tifton Cash or a soap opera, and listening to Tifton Cash reminded her of sitting in church as a child with her mother, unwrapping slice after slice of Wrigley's Spearmint gum. Dr. Cash told the audience that was his real name, though that coincidence of his name wouldn't stop him, he said, from preaching on the blessing of prosperity. And he did: he said that invoking Jesus's name was our claim ticket to the promises of God, which include material wealth.

Tifton Cash said you had to pray to God with your claim ticket knowing that you already had the things you were asking for, because Jesus had gotten them for you when he died. They were all just waiting, like items you'd pawned waiting in a pawn shop, for you to get them. You needed the ticket and God had the money ready. The ticket was the words. Cash said you had to pray using phrases from the Bible—"speaking to God in his own language," as Cash put it. God understands our words, of course, Cash said, but his word was perfect while ours was not.

Ef decided she would look in the Bible at home every day and find phrases to remember, though she would have to be careful. Her mother's Bible held all the family records: births, deaths, piles of news stories and obituaries and old Mass cards with lit hearts. Allusions to troubles long prayed over and long past slid out whenever she opened it. And her parents, Catholics, accepted her no longer attending church, but listening to evangelists on TV would be beyond what they could tolerate without scolding her. *Pray the blessed rosary,* her dad would say, shaking the beads he kept in his left pocket.

Of course, those words too were words God chose.

She also liked a woman preacher, an older woman named Becky Fellow. Becky Fellow wore pantsuits and had hair lacquered into a reddish orb around her head. Ef noticed that Becky Fellow had more and more plastic surgery as her shows went on, most obviously around the mouth. Her mouth ended up looking like Jack Nicholson's in his Joker makeup. It stretched way too far up her cheeks, yanked and sharp at the corners, like a leg-hold trap or an open pair of scissors. This was not plastic surgery as the Crawleys did it. The strange look did not put Ef off Fellow's preaching, though. That mouth seemed to cut off each thing she said: this is the truth, here I bite it off.

"You know what's normal for a believer!" Fellow said one day. "Peace!" Her mouth clamped down on the word and gave weight to the silence, a silence unsettled as a doorbell that suddenly stops ringing. Ef understood there could be no other answer.

Another preacher she watched said he came from Puerto Rico, like her father, though unlike her slight and accented father, he spoke like an American—like a man from the American South—and stood tall and large. The preacher was pale, "Cauca-Rican" as her father would put it. She tuned into him—Dr. Vernon Light Johnson—now, in a room with wet towels everywhere, twists of foil and a musk of marijuana. She had to get the smell out; the next guests would complain.

"This ordinariness is beneath you," Light boomed when she turned up the television. "It is beneath you and who you were created to be." Dr. Light stood behind his gold pulpit, dressed beautifully, as always—a blue suit with a hint of purple, a color picked up by a purple pocket square and the stripes in his tie. He had an enormous, gleaming, bald head and a touch of mustache.

Dr. Light, who also assured his audience of the reality of his name ("I just translated it from the Spanish into the American," he told them), had a habit of preaching while he slowly turned all the way around. He first made a quarter turn to the right; then another one to the back, so the camera filmed the rear of his suit and the back of his head, creased and rift and aglow. Then he turned another quarter turn to his left, and finally back to the front again. Ef loved this about Light, the way as he preached he seemed to turn into a celestial body, rotating in its orbit. It added some mysterious truth to his words, that they blew and pulled him around from the inside. Though she glanced up at the screen today in the midst of setting some air freshener bombs and realized for the first time that he had audience members seated to the sides of him and behind him, and the camera just didn't follow him around as he turned to those people.

Dr. Light said, with his back to her, "Your dreams will tell you who you really are."

When Ef had done what she could with the room, she went to turn off the television, grabbing the remote. Just as her finger descended on the button, though, Dr. V. Light Johnson shifted his eyes, looking right at her. "I am not standing here talking to you like any other man talking through the television. One word pouring after another, no. The Lord gives you ears to hear," and Light made as if to root through his ear with a wide finger. "The Lord will open your ears and he will plug them up. If I say something and it doesn't grab you, it's not for you. If it's for you it won't let you go."

When Ef came home from work her mother had her feet up in the Stratolounger with a doily on the back.

"Bo-Bean!" she said. "Could you get me the channel changer?"

Next to her mother's chair was a gold lamp with a naked lady in it surrounded by wires of metal that ran slowly and continuously with beads of warm oil. Her school friends and her mother all called it the Naked Lady in the Rain Lamp, but the school friends said the phrase in an entirely different way than her mother. When Ef was a child, sensitive to the feelings of things, she shivered for the gold woman when the lamp was switched off.

Now the lamp mostly irritated her, the way it irritated her that her father called what they used to wipe dishes a *rag* and her mother called it a *moppin'*, neither of them using the right word, dishtowel. Her father ate plantains and sometimes, inexplicably, dribbled soy sauce on them. He and her mother used words the way other Americans would not, putting "the" before the wrong things: *we're going to have the meatballs and the spaghetti, we're going to have the arroz.*

Actually, her mother often called it not spaghetti but something like *a-shpaget*. When Ef was a teenager, she would say, *Ma, nobody talks like that.* The pronunciations, the "the's" all over the place. And her mother would say, "I do," an answer that filled her with a pitying anger that might have been an angry pity.

"Ma," she said now, "Why do you call me that?"

"Oh, you know, that old song, banana-bana-fo-fana, meeny-meeny-bo-beanie," her mother half sang, "or whatever."

When Ef went into the kitchen she noticed the faucet gleaming. Her mother had scrubbed it with a toothbrush, after leaving it draped in a paper towel soaked in white vinegar, as Ef had taught her. Her mother liked to tell her sister in their daily phone call that Ef "cleaned like a wizard!"

Ef's mother always started her phone calls to her sister with something like how to clean a faucet, and then her brows contracted and she said words like, "You're kidding! Well, goddamn!" and burst into the unintelligible dialect of Italian her family spoke. Her mother's Southern Italian sounded hard, consonantal, like German. When Ef was in school, as soon as kids heard where her mother came from, they mocked her to Ef by adding "a's" and "o's" to the end of everything: *izzata your-a backa-packa?* It puzzled Ef until she heard other people mimic Italians on TV, because the mockery sounded nothing like her mom—if anything, it sounded closer to her father's accent. Her mother's hard consonants could have come out of the mouth of Becky Fellow: final, sharp as a heel on the floor.

Her father's accent consisted of a beautiful lilting and a slight *sh* sound on some s's.

"How long are you going to clean for a living?" he'd asked her the other day. He saw no benefit in her job and wanted her to return to school.

Her mother loved opera, and called it by its Italian name, *la lirica*. You could not speak to her mother on Sunday afternoon; she'd have the radio on, a broadcast from some opera company in New York, and if she spoke her mother hissed, "Filomena, la lirica!" in a voice that made la lirica sound like a stoning. Her father had learned to love it too, particularly Rossini. It was sometimes hard to explain to people that her mother and father loved opera but still had little education and not much money.

"People think you're fancy," she told her mother once, and her mother threw the moppin' over her shoulder and said, "Fancy would be the symphony."

Both of her parents had predicted great things for Ef growing up, but a lot of their faith seemed based on what they never quit believing was her astonishing height: so much more than could be expected, and a badge of greatness. They measured her weekly and her height became something like her family's stock market, with giddy bull markets when the line rose. Actually, Ef could only be seen as tall in relation to the pair of them. She ended up a shade below five foot six and petite—almost her father's height, and many inches above her mother's, but still. She could never convince them that as American girls went she was average.

"A tall girl like you, you can model even," her mother told her in high school.

That one statement (*If it's not for you*) by Dr. Light changed the way Ef listened to her preachers, because it in fact did not let her go. It rang through her head as she fell asleep and seeped into her mind in the morning. *If it's not . . .*

It wound around her as she stood in her closet looking at the shoes she'd stolen.

If it's meant for you . . . but what exactly was meant for her? The message was only about remembering the message.

Ef started tuning in Dr. Light whenever she could—as soon as she arrived in a room at work; at home, if her parents happened to be out. As she drove to work, she no longer imagined her elevator ride at the end of the day, her daily entrance into the life of the pampered. She imagined the television, that today another hint might be thrown out: something about her life, something about what she could claim.

She heard preaching on the stain of sin with her rubber-gloved hand in a toilet, agitating Rust-Out with a chaser of bleach. The hotel left out cards for guests pledging to do environmentally responsible cleaning; none of this pledge they really followed. "That stain will never come free without redemption," said Light, and as he said those words the reddish bloom on the porcelain dissolved from the walls of the bowl into water. Which was a sign, Ef thought. But the lifting of the stain with Clorox rather than something natural was part of a lie, a sin perhaps: a sign too.

While she crouched over the tub by the window at the hotel, Dr. Light told her about the trials in her life.

"You say, you're the one who gets caught, you're the one who gets fired for sneaking a smoke behind the warehouse, when everyone else sneaks out there to have that same smoke," said Light. "You are the woman who can't let another man give her a wink or a look without your husband seeing, you are the man who can't say once his boss is a damn fool without that damn fool creeping up behind him." He paused. "Maybe you were the child who got a look at his father's dirty magazines just *once*, who stole a dollar out of her mother's purse just *once*, the kid who got caught and got the whipping of your life. Your brothers and your sisters were laughing into their hands." Light looked out over the audience. "Am I right?"

And everyone listening, one after another, nodded, though Ef thought, they couldn't all be that one person.

"You were that scapegoat, you tell yourself. Maybe for your coworkers, your friends, your family, you were always that sacrifice.

"You say to me, Doctor, my coworkers get away with it. Like my brothers and my sisters used to get away with it." Light paused, lifted his Bible, looked into the camera. "Let me tell you why the Lord has chosen you to be found out, to be that goat led to the altar for slaughter. He loves you. You can't get away with what others get away with because you belong to God." Light raised his Bible higher. "Here it is in Hebrews: whom the Lord loveth he chasteneth. He chastens and scourges whom he loves."

Ef's heart beat faster. Though as she considered the words she couldn't decide how they spoke to her: she'd gotten away with so much in her life. She had stolen clothing and nobody seemed to notice. She had lied to Tom and taken advantage of his generosity. She had really lied without words every time she rode that elevator in her nice clothes.

Her parents had never whipped her. They indulged her. The evidence seemed to say God didn't care about her at all.

Or maybe God wanted her to steal, wanted her to doubt herself, so that she would tune in and listen.

Two rooms later, Ef still watched Light, but his earlier words—their tone of significance—kept ringing. Perhaps she was about to be tried, terribly tried. Ef remembered the thought of pushing the cart of her life, room to room, till age brought her to an end. And she had tried to shop for clothes, but found that, away from the hotel, her sense of herself was practical and prosaic: *where would I wear this?* she asked herself, putting everything back that she tried on. Was that her trial? It didn't feel that way. She had no family of her own, no children to support, unlike most of the maids. She could not call herself trapped.

Still, Ef developed a stubborn image in her head, of Light pushing her cart, Becky Fellow and Tifton Cash pulling it. She decided that that image meant they were telling her something, something that she needed to hear.

Ef's hotel had a small library on the third floor. It was Ef's week to keep it clean. The room had the look of a library on a television show: a lot of woodwork, open cases of books with statuettes—a boy dressed as a chimney sweep, a ballet dancer on her toe. Vases, vaguely Asian looking. Cushioned chairs. Most guests appreciated that the library existed—or they murmured their appreciation as they checked in—but did not use it. Ef splayed the feather duster along the shelves, put away the few books left lying on the arms of chairs. Whenever she cleaned the library she wondered if she ought to read more, but today, as she looked at books with promising titles, she couldn't quite bring herself to borrow them. She read the words on the flaps and laid the books down.

When May realized her long-gone sister Edna was returning...

When Sam realized it was his bullet that had taken out Ernest in that hail of fire...

It was always the "when" that struck her as dishonest. There was only a *now*, and it never had that kind of shine to it.

She picked up a magazine that had Cate Crawley on the cover. There were many magazines featuring Cate here, recently dropped off. Ef's boss had mentioned Cate would be coming through town soon. Ef knew that this magazine, too, would be false, but in a very different way, in a way that everyone winkingly admitted. She stuffed the magazine into her purse.

Ef thought of Tom, who had met her as Celeste, wearing other people's clothes. And yet she felt at one point at least he had really seen her. Seen her, though walking by her at her cart he would have no idea who she was, would not know her by her name or her face.

For now we see through a glass darkly. All the preachers loved that phrase. And it was true, and it formed the logic by which Ef did not grudge the preachers their theatrical gestures, their buoyant hallelujahs and their tears. She did not even mind in the Crawleys their stunt-like fights, the way Cate for instance didn't just get mad at J-lord for stepping on her wet pedicure, but stunned him with a right hook (and oh did this gesture get hashed over for what felt like forever on TV, on doctor-driven talk shows, on 24-hour news shows. Was it domestic abuse? Did we forgive domestic abuse coming from a small curvy woman?)

The Crawley clothes that hardly seemed like clothes, more like bindings bandaging their secrets, the vulnerable bits of the body things go into and out of. Everyone sees each other through a glass darkly, so in order to be seen everyone has to prance wildly, in the most exaggerated ways and the loudest colors, in order to be seen at all.

The problem was, Ef thought, discovering your own particular exaggeration, the prancing that would work for you: that was hard.

Later, Ef found Dr. Light on TV again. She cleaned some common areas after the library, then headed to the upper rooms, and caught Light at the end of his show. It was an old episode. Light was thinner, still had a horseshoe of hair on his head, and did not dress as nicely. He wore a plain navy suit, with a white shirt, and no pocket square. Ef noticed he did not yet have his diamond wedding ring, which was rectangular, shiny, larger than a Fisherman's Friend cough drop.

"You tell them with your words and you tell them with your body that it is OK!" Light was shouting. He had made a fist with one hand and shook it at the audience. Light blustered even more back then; he seemed to have less confidence. "You tell the fornicator that it is OK! You tell the adulterer that it is OK! You even tell the blasphemer that it is OK!

"Would you watch a man approach our Lord and then slap our Lord as hard as he could on the cheek? Would you stand there and let him put the mark of his hand on the blessed cheek?" Light slapped the air and the audience shook their heads. Ef found herself shaking her head *no* too, passionately, wanting to get out from under Light's suspicion. "Would you allow him to take from Jesus his robe, his few coins?

"Yet you allow the fornicators, the adulterers, the blasphemers to slap him right in that blessed face—again and again." Light slowed down, rhythmically batting the air with his hand, open palm, then closed fist, "and again." He whispered, "The sinner is the thief of our Lord and the thug of our Lord. He steals redemption and harms the flesh our Lord took on for our sake. We must protect our Lord. Say amen."

In the next room, Becky Fellow told Ef that once she accepted the Lord the Lord would fill her, tell her what to do. Ef closed her eyes and told the Lord that she accepted him—she accepted him very much, she said—and she forced herself to imagine the inside of her standing open, like a dresser to be filled. Yet she did not feel she knew what to do.

The woman had a bathrobe on—dark—and a scarf cowled around her head, covering almost all of her face. She had put no *Do Not Disturb* sign on the door and didn't respond to a knock, so Ef had pushed the door open and wheeled in, catching a glimpse: the woman's cowl snugged around a face red and swollen, eyes blackened all the way around, scabs arcing down her cheeks. Her skin had a ruddy wetness; it seemed to seep blood. As the woman spoke to Ef, she turned—like Light—her face to the wall.

"Could you please just clean the bathroom for me," the woman mumbled, her voice absorbed by the wall. "The rest'll be fine."

Ef startled all over her body; yanked along the line of her nerves. The raw face turning to the wall, the cowled head hanging.

Could this be her challenge, her something to do?

"Do you need anything?" she asked the woman, though she couldn't imagine what she might give her.

Her first thought: here stood a woman beaten. Perhaps she hid from her abuser. Her second thought: here stood a penitent, someone who had done something terrible, muffling herself away from the world in a hotel, the damned face taboo, the hotel the closest thing she could find to a cloister.

The woman mumbled something that had the word "recovery" in it and Ef realized with relief and a selfish disappointment that the woman had just come from a face lift. The first week after you looked ghastly, and many women spent those days in hotels. By the time the woman checked out she would wear a scarf to hide the scabs and there would still be swelling, darkening around the eyes. But she would look better, and if Ef saw her later—at the hotel restaurant, or somewhere in town—she would look remade: fresh, taut, clean. From a penitent she would have become almost a Crawley.

And that suggested the opposite thought: at some point the Crawley women, all of them so in love with plastic surgery, had looked like this. Ef thought of them the last time she saw the show, their skintight clothing and burnished faces. Cate Crawley could widen her eyes and purse her lips without her face moving.

Cate's face—all their faces—so remarkably finished, impossible for anything to affect or penetrate, and yet at some time these had opened themselves, seeped blood. Their beauty was a series of healed, small wounds. You opened all the way, in order that you might close completely. It felt like something Ef could learn.

Becky Fellow, too, had looked like this woman. Her skin was tight, pulling the skewed mouth after it like the moon's forcing a crisp wave.

As Ef cleaned the woman's bathroom, she found a business card dropped on the tile. It had a photo of a middle-aged woman, dark-haired and smiling hard, and the job title *Realtor*. Ef could see within the photo a face, of which the woman in the room now wore the funhouse mirror version. The card had a cell phone number. Ef put it in her pocket, for no real reason.

Later Ef chose to send the woman a message.

She borrowed the cell phone that belonged to the concierge's desk, tapping into it *You will be very beautiful soon*. Then she hit Send. She imagined the beep, the distracted woman pulling back her cowl to read the text from a number she did not recognize, the warmth of sudden happiness hidden by her flushed rawness. Ef imagined the woman then selecting the person she would most want to get this message from, going through in her head the reasons her guess was the correct one. It was like handing her a dream she could plug her own dream into.

Ef wanted to name and claim her prosperity and whatever else might be waiting for her, and she wanted to talk to God in language God would particularly like. Light also went into that riff, on praying using the words in the Bible in the proper order and way.

"There's a lot of noise up there!" he said, "so you show him you know him and his word—'Lord, according to Isaiah, by Jesus's stripes I am already healed.' That should be your prayer when you're sick. The Bible will give you the words you need. Paradise is a strange and distant country and you are a lost traveler. The Bible is like your phrase book for the Lord."

It had made Ef feel good to send the text message. Perhaps this could be her ministry: the secrets she knew about people who found their sanctuary in hotels, the words she could use that would surprise them, change them with their truth.

That weekend Ef had the Saturday shift. She entered a room as the man in it was leaving. He wore a polo shirt and had a neat, thin mustache. In the room, she found a wedding ring on the side table, with several Kleenex spread out on top of it. Later she noticed the man again, coming into the hotel in the late afternoon with a woman at his side. The two of them had their heads down, laughing. The woman reached out a hand toward him: a left hand, ringless. She had bland features that could have been pretty, but she had dyed her hair an almost white shade of blond. It bobbed to her chin, white-blond from black roots, and made her features exaggeratedly plain, much as a harsh light would have.

They both held themselves carefully six inches apart, the same distance at the feet as at the shoulders, like magnets whose charges opposed. Their care made Ef wonder. She checked the rooms chart: the man in thirty-two was listed as a single.

A tryst. She knew from the ring and the couple's self-aware distance.

Like the cowled woman, the man left his business cards in his room. Ef retrieved one and waited, again, until the concierge stepped away. At first she typed into the small screen, *I saw that you left your wedding ring* but she backspaced that out. Only the maids could have seen the ring, and her ministry wouldn't work if she let herself be known.

Instead she typed in *Sinners in the hands of an angry God.*

Ef had heard Light say the phrase and she liked it—just the sound of it—so she hit Send. She imagined the words striking him like a blow to a gong, and him rethinking his life in the ringing. Perhaps someone should have done this for her, the first time she stole.

She wondered if anyone would try to chase down the concierge's phone number. Unlikely that they'd choose to embarrass themselves this way.

Ef saw Tom again when she had forgotten Tom existed. When Tom ceased to play a role in her imagination, then he reappeared. She rode the elevator with him. He wore his suit and she glimpsed the watch on his wrist, the long fair lashes. As she'd predicted, he did not recognize her. He had his hand in his pocket and his eyes bored into the floor numbers on the panel. He fingered a room key.

Tom exited the elevator on the second floor. Ef pushed her cart out and left it in the hallway, padding a little way behind him. He never turned but took out his key card and let himself into room 216. It was morning, around eight o'clock. The room did not appear on her list of rooms to clean.

When she later bumped into a man—quick bump in a hallway, her face down and a mechanical *sorry*—she was overwhelmed by the sense that this collision had happened before but been transformed somehow. It was and wasn't deja-vu. And then she saw the restless eyes, the eyelashes: long, curling, like the silks from an ear of corn.

Tom wore a wig, shoulder-length, black, shagged, and fluffy. He had dark pencil around his eyes and lips filled in with black. His shirt glittered and stretched unbuttoned to the waist, revealing butter-colored hair. The shirt vee-ed above tight white pants and high white boots with black grommets down the side. The overall effect was of a member of a band like Kiss, without their white face paint. Maybe also a touch of Elvis. Though the look wasn't particularly well done, the wig too boy-band and wiggy, the pale chest somehow embarrassed by it all. Ef's eyes stayed downcast as Tom passed her and she noticed a huge bulge at his crotch. It looked like he'd stuffed a sock down there, as she'd heard rockers sometimes do, but it could just be a well-endowed Tom in tight pants. He walked with a long stride and his thumbs stuck into the pants' waist, through the halls of a hotel that hosted celebrities passing through from time to time. Tom's was an entirely different walk than the one she'd seen, with long strides and an exaggerated heel-toe hit to the floor. It didn't match the movement with which he had crushed her foot.

Ef followed him with her eyes, trying to match this image of the man she saw with the image of the man she'd eaten dinner with. The two men both came together and did not. This was a shaped and particular identity, like the lovers who found their passion when dressed up as maids.

Ef had let herself into Tom's room.

She knocked and waited, and waited, and opened the door slowly. Lunchtime, and an empty floor. She locked his door with the chain lock from the inside, so if his proper maid came, she could not get in until Ef let her in. Ef had invented a story about feeling sick as she walked by, needing a bathroom. It would be fine as long as Tom stayed away; the maids never turned on one another.

Tom's room was neat, no suitcase visible, bare surfaces. A cosmetic bag in the bathroom, zipped. Ef went through it and found a thick black pencil and black lipstick, like Halloween makeup. In the closet were studded black boots with a high heel, placed carefully parallel.

In a dresser drawer she found his wallet. It spilled a few old business cards, a card from an ice cream parlor that stamped each purchase with a cone-shaped stamp. School photos of two grade-school children, smiling so hard they seemed to want to drive their lips away. Their distinctive butter-blond hair identified them as his. In another photo the children sat to the side of a blond, sweatered woman perching with Tom on a log of driftwood, his arms around her, and her hand on his thigh.

Ef had no idea how to feel. So she kept looking.

And found in Tom's trash can a program for a conference in Tucson, one that had just ended, so perhaps he checked in while stealing a few extra days for himself. The conference was called *Caring for our Shepherds*. Sessions had names like "Listening to the Listener" and "Can We Have Pastoral Excellence in the Face of Trauma?" It was, the introductory words explained, a conference for pastors who ministered to other pastors, because a pastor's work was stressful and full of heartache and they too needed help. One session covered how to ensure our shepherds kept upholding our values for their flocks. The *our* and the *values* sounded ominous. Ef had never imagined such a job as a ministry for ministers, though it made sense.

Ef thought so much about shepherds and flocks. She had not thought of any of this.

Time passed and Ef heard movement in the hallway and knew she needed to leave. The drawer hung open and rooting through it would get her fired, just when she had discovered her preachers, a mission, the phone at the concierge desk. But she could not let go of the photos in her hand. She felt like a worm squirming on a hook, sensing maybe that its actions would cause the thing to happen that it feared would happen. But there are laws in this universe: if on a hook, you squirm.

Finally she threw the photo down into the dresser drawer, unlatched the door, and left. Guests came and went but no one paid her any mind. She headed for the elevator to go back to her scheduled rooms. She could not get Tom in his wig and the woman in the photo out of her head; she kept putting them together, Tom as she had seen him first, long arms wrapped around the smaller woman, their heads angled together—her three-quarter profile from one side facing his three-quarter profile from the other. And the two of them in love.

Perhaps the woman loved him completely in any clothing. Probably. And it was his choice to come to the Mariposa to be clear and anonymous in a fantasy caught in beloved clothes and a beloved wig. Just as Ef chose to be clear and anonymous at the end of each day in her good clothes.

Ef tried to imagine what Tifton Cash would say, what Becky Fellow and most importantly, Vernon Light Johnson would say. Light would have some book of the Bible that would comment on this very situation, some obscure name, Hosea, Baruch. The judgment would not go in Tom's favor. There would not be words from the Bible Tom could use to explain himself to the Lord, in his bold erotic clothes. He would have to use his own words, and those, Cash and Light would say, God did not wish to recognize.

Later Ef picked up the phone at the concierge's desk. She had Tom's cell phone number and tried to imagine what she might say. As usual she wore her coat buttoned around her uniform, so if anyone saw her standing there, the person would assume she was a guest waiting for the concierge—who luckily spent a ridiculous amount of time away from her desk.

She tried to imagine a message and felt the pressure of Light's and the other preachers' words to tell Tom he should be upholding our values to his sheep. But when she thought of him—the wife, the children, the high boots—she couldn't. Becky Fellow had given a talk yesterday called "If you want to walk on water you gotta get out of the boat!" She dragged a white rowboat onstage and got women from the audience to huddle together in it, pretending to be afraid. The women wailed and waved their hands in the air. Then Becky Fellow stepped out of the boat and the frightened women stepped out too.

You are out of the boat now, she wrote, then erased it. It would only make sense to her.

She did not want to put Tom in front of the preachers or anyone else in judgment. Ef understood that Tom embraced with courage something he felt he needed to do, something outside what he'd probably think of as his life.

She thought of the way she felt sharing cigarettes with other women, that warm flood that centered just outside of what her mother used to call her *down there*, her *little cookie*, the things she thought about when she touched herself to climax, things probably far from *our values*. How hard to find a way to live without hiding. How she worked in a place that, like the Crawleys, both hid and exposed.

And then as usual her day wheeled its hours: room upon room. The slob-guest wave had ended. Back to form. Thrown towels assuming geologic shapes, sprawls of cosmetics that promised to retool, relift, regenerate. Re, re, re. Ef went from room to room every half an hour, winding up time like a clock, but in all cases erased the evidence anything had happened in that room, so more like a clock winding backward. Ef left late and went home in her uniform.

Her mother lay back in the dark, by the turned-off lamp, its little tears of oil stilled along the wires.
"Mina!"
Ef realized her mother had been sleeping.
"Don't get up, Ma." She tried to walk quietly to her room, but her mother turned the lamp on, and the oil slowly began pearling and rolling again.
"Mina, are you home early from work? Do you need a lunch?" Ef realized her mother had been sleeping a long time. Her ma pulled the lever that brought the chair into a sitting position. She turned her head and looked at the lamp for a while, with a smile of pleasure, as if she'd never quite appreciated it before.
"Ah, Mina," her mother said, and looked at her watch, still with that look of happiness. "It's late. Time to peel some potatoes." She reached a finger through the wires of flowing oil to touch the gold lady in the center of the lamp.
"Are you tickling the lady in the lamp, Ma?"
"What, Beanie?" Her mother turned to her.
"Nothing. Ma."
"You never come home in that uniform," her mother said, still regarding her. "You don't look half bad in it. A shame it's got that stupid apron. Isn't that for like a French maid or something?"

"I don't know." Ef smiled, a smile that was a little exaggerated; she wanted her mother to know she loved her.

Because Ef had thought suddenly that, like the Crawley grandmother, her mother would die some day: that the day would come much sooner than she could imagine, no matter when it was, and her mother's touch, her warmth, would leak off the lamp and never return to it again. The lamp would end up in some resale store and then be a joke in somebody's man cave or college dorm room. An irrational anger took hold of her. *How would my ma know it's funny? It's the only lamp like this she's ever seen!*

Seeing anything only once would make it magical. Like the items she stole from hotel rooms.

"You always look good," Ef's mother said, "you look like you," and Ef let a half-formed thought that had been growing all afternoon through: what if Tom had recognized her? What if he recognized her early on, or today when they bumped together, as a woman who once pretended to be a wealthy businesswoman but was really a maid. His indifference would have been a remarkable kindness.

Ef remembered a line of poetry from a college English course: *you must change your life.* Light said this, and Becky Fellow, and Tifton Cash. All the Crawley family members hurled versions of this sentiment at one another and at their boyfriends and husbands. It seemed to be the one thing everyone could agree on—preachers; poets; Crawleys. They all mouthed it at her through their particular glass. But how would she change, and to whom?

CC: Copy Cat

She rested her forehead on the steering wheel of her car, just for a second, her cool, static, almost foreign-feeling skin kissing cousin to the leather. She had just had a long meeting with the network execs and her producer and their Q consultants. These were the chunks of her day when the camera could not follow her; she had on no makeup and decided to stay on her own for a while, heading the car toward her gym. Hair up, shades on, colorless features receding, she'd mostly go unnoticed. Her eyes without false lashes and thick makeup felt light, the lid flying weightless off the pupil.

It was, as these weekly meetings always were, a lot to take in. Candy and Carlotta continued trending down in their Q scores, and before yanking their spinoff, the head of programming wanted to try one more thing: sending them to lesser-known locations and incorporating travel information into the show. They threw out possible locations: Molokai in Hawaii, Vanua Levu in Fiji.

"If people want to see Paris they'll watch Rick Steves," the head of programming said. "This way people get vacation ideas, they get beaches, they get tits and ass." He always said *tits and ass* when talking to Cate, not *T and A*, the standard abbreviation, as if in doing so he flattered her dignity. Though he always used the family abbreviation for *Crawleys Coming On: CCO,* or just *Cuck*. "Maybe we can have them show up with a paunch, do some diet tips too. Tie it in with Cuck."

"They're both signed on to Nutrilose, they can't do any other diet," Cate reminded him patiently.

"Fucking Nutrilose." They had this exchange all the time.

The audience wanted fewer love scenes between her and J-lord; they were miffed at J and wanted her to cut him off. Cassie, though, had a Fox news anchor as her new boyfriend. He and Cassie rolled in her satin sheets and viewers tweeted *Hypocrite!* at him. *Family values, yeah.* They loved it, digging with big spoons into the ice cream sundaes of their indignation.

Cate realized her eyes were tired and that, given their lack of makeup, she could rub them, so she did. The Raw Girls had Egyptian blood through their father Jerry, something else Cate needed to handle carefully—their skin, easily darkened, read as exotic, a plus, but some viewers could find them too ethnic. They stressed the family's Christianity.

J-lord remained popular overall, as did Candy and Carlotta's boyfriends du jour, Andre and Alan. J-lord was the kind of guy who ordered bottle after bottle of Hennessy when he went out, then needed attention from whatever women happened to be around. He would sleep with them if he got drunk enough. Cate had a forgiveness scene with him every month or so. Andre tended to want to hit guys he thought looked at Candy the wrong way, and Alan, a golfer, whined to Carlotta whenever he lost a game. She took his head in her lap and told him he was her champ.

At the gym Cate straddled an exercise bike. She had a personal trainer and home gym, but she liked this too from time to time, being one in a group, spinning and spinning, no cameras. As she began to sweat, she felt a ring of heat around her forehead, where the Botox didn't reach, and bits of hair working free only to dampen and glue themselves to her cheeks.

She looked in the mirror at the woman on the next bike over, not bad looking, she thought to herself, her hair also parted sharply in the middle, stretched into a ponytail, not quite enough lip, wide eyes that could use some help, a cheek that could be filled in with dark contour to create the effect of cheekbones . . .

Then Cate realized she was staring at herself, and in thinking through improvements to the stranger just imagining herself as she'd actually be, as soon as she got to her next appointment and found her stylists and was *done*. She imagined what her critics would write, if they knew she couldn't recognize her unmade-up self in a mirror: the three C's, the Cooked-Up Counterfeit Crawleys, one columnist called them.

In her heart she understood that that was wrong. The Cate she would become when she got home was as real as this one: realer, as this Cate still had the reworked nose and jaws, the skin frozen at age twenty due to ongoing injections, hair dyed deep red. And even if she'd never had knife touched to skin, that untouched Cate would never be as real as the televised one, the Cate of her imagination, the Cate that existed for her fans. That Cate could get on television and say what was on her mind—run down her ungrateful bitch sisters, her insatiable cow of a mother, as she called them, part of the language of the show—achieving an honesty in her life no one else in the universe could match.

Next Cate had an appearance with her medium. Her film crew and hair and makeup people would meet her at Heidi's house, a Tuscan-style villa in Calabasas. Cate had first heard about Heidi from a frenemy on her housewife spinoff *Bel Air Lunch* and scheduled a visit during a slow period on Cuck. The episode was wildly popular, and Heidi now had her own show, *Clairvoying*. Cate was a producer and got a percentage of the revenue; it was her idea to turn clairvoyant into a verb. In return, she contracted to have a filmed visit once a month.

Cate's people glammed her in her car. She rang the bell—of course, Heidi herself was glamming inside—and Heidi yanked open the door and greeted Cate, head thrown forward in enthusiastic hello. Cate's director hated the gesture. "You look like you're going to eat her," he told Heidi, and they reshot.

Inside, Heidi had her own film crew jerking cameras around and lowering fuzzy sound booms toward them. The reading would appear on both shows, with different cuts and angles. Cate felt surrounded by too many eyes. She looked away from all of them, relaxed into the sofa, a dark green chosen to offset her red hair.

Cate said, "Say, I know you'll do your miracles today, Heidi. And you're redoing your dining room."

"It was too gold."

"Gold can be so extra."

Heidi had black hair that scooped down her cheeks and around her face, like a helmet, and dark eyes. She wore an astonishing number of rings, silver and long enough to reach her first knuckle, so that her fingers looked as if they were made of steel. Out of them curved pointed nails painted in different dark colors. Android hands, thought Cate. Fortyish, Heidi had a neck and hands that looked older. Heidi nodded toward her crew's cameras, to begin her reading. She lifted her chin and squinched her eyes hard shut. Once she started clairvoying, she began many sentences with "acknowledging," and her voice changed to a singsong.

"Acknowledging we now open the book of Cate. Acknowledging the spirits are telling you to notice the twentieth of August," she sang. "The spirits are telling you someone's talking dirt behind your back."

As of course more than one someone was. Cate paid them to.

Heidi tapped her astonishing fingers against her glass coffee table. They sounded like coins spilling on the Formica counter of an old diner. This was odd; Heidi valued little, but she protected her hands. "Acknowledging someone wants to talk to you. Someone who's not here in your life yet."

Cate widened her eyes toward her. Heidi couldn't venture into the area of children, or anything that could be interpreted that way. Cate didn't allow it.

"Acknowledging it's not a child," said Heidi quickly. "It's a person. A person with something to give you."

The session felt lame, so Cate fed the medium some ideas.

"Is it a living person? Or passed on? Could it be my grandmother?" Viewers loved the grandmother sessions.

"It could be," said Heidi. "Probably. Acknowledging probably."

She tried so hard to anticipate what Cate wanted. Suddenly it occurred to Cate that Heidi was a real person. The awareness felt like a fall into something: Heidi was a living, breathing, thinking person, but talked and gestured much of the time in a world scripted for her by Cate Crawley.

Cate's grandmother had died eight months before this. The programming people wanted to film the women visiting their grandma in the hospital, at first. The head of programming loved the idea, and Will her director insisted on bringing the crew in with them on their first hospital visit, but as soon as he looked around the room, he said *Nuts to this* and left.

Now Tita's chin wore a brush of steel whiskers and she'd developed coppery spots on her face, like pennies pressed into her skin. Her hair matted to her head in the back and stuck up in front and she had milky cataracts on both eyes, giving her a pale blue stare that was distant yet still at times fierce and aware. Tita had vascular dementia, dementia from a series of strokes.

CC: Copy Cat

Tita wore a hospital gown and she kept kicking off her covers, leaving herself exposed. It was a shock to see her grandmother's body. Her skin had kept its role as covering but was no longer container, falling free in folds from the bony tips of her skeleton, and her pubic area sunk under a gray frizz.

Tita seemed terrified of dying and rose to the spoons of tuna salad and applesauce the nurse's aides held out to her, saying *Am I being a good girl? a good girl?* as she sucked in the food.

After her stint in the hospital, Tita went to the dementia ward of a nursing home. Cate visited the most, not just to see Tita but also to get away, the way she'd sometimes sit far too long in the bathroom at home, away from the camera crews, the boom that hovered over her and her family, catching their voices.

There was a reminder here in the nursing home: someday she'd live fully inside her own body again, back in her inborn physicality, until that physicality like a nervous horse threw her off, as it was doing to her grandmother.

Was this a hard thought? Sometimes Cate went cold inside, looking at her Tita. Other times she surveyed the old woman's face and hair and body, thinking of each piece of herself she could someday, finally, let go. The skin hanging pouchlike off her. The sensation didn't feel happy, but it had a note of resignation to it that was not without sweetness.

Cate reminded her grandmother of foods they used to eat together ("Remember those Lucky Charms? Don't you wish we had some Lucky Charms?" of a cereal her Tita snuck her when she was a little girl) and sang lullabies in her thin voice. One day she heard herself saying, "Tita, remember how I used to say I was going to be a doctor?"—a fact she'd almost forgotten about herself, that she'd once wanted this. She'd gotten through a semester of college, back before the show. She loved her science classes, anatomy, the pipes and islands of the body. No one outside the family knew these things about Cate—her mind, as her agent put it, not being her key asset. And the change in her ambitions did not mean much to Cate. She had always imagined herself as a practitioner who'd see person after person and tell them things about themselves they didn't know. She'd be impressive to them. But only so many people—maybe twenty—could see her in a day. Only as many as she had fingers and toes.

Tita died in the nursing home of an infection called C diff, *clostridium difficile*. C diff proved to be an awful death, with wasting diarrhea. On the show they used just seven or eight minutes' footage from the funeral, reaction shots of Jerry—who had divorced their mother a long time ago—and the Crawley women as each in turn teared up. A brief shot of the minister. Cate had gone through the footage with the film editor and thought hard about what clips to use.

Cate had executive producer status on the show and had the contractual right to edit and approve all footage before it aired. Her sisters and mother had input, but Cate looked at everything and made final decisions. She often went through the dailies—the raw footage from each day's shooting—with Will and/or the film editor. With a scene that didn't work as first filmed, she ordered reshoots. Her mother and sisters could also call for reshoots, and when they did, it was almost always because they didn't like the way they looked. A production assistant would go through the original and type up the dialogue, then they'd do it all again, repeating the dialogue (they could change it if they wanted) and trying different clothes and makeup and new lighting and angles.

Certain rules were basic: never show the Crawley household's maids, or the cook (though viewers loved to see the family in chauffeured limos or private planes, it bothered them to no end—and Cate would hear about it—to see maids picking up in their house, or a cook making dinner).

J-lord's proposal to Cate had been reshot four times. It was a popular episode and dramatic. J-lord surprised Cate (actually both Will and her mother had told Cate ahead of time, but J didn't know that she knew) by getting down on one knee in their bedroom, a room he'd filled for the occasion with bouquets of lilies and red candles the shade of her hair. He knelt, holding out the ring, so expensive it had arrived by Brink's truck. She came home from a laser appointment and walked in the bedroom as he held out the box with the ten-carat oblong diamond. He had *Marry Me* written on the mirror in Cate's favorite red lipstick.

J said the words, too, when she walked in, from his kneeling position: *Cate, will you marry me?* Then he said, *I want to spend my life with you.*

The problem was that Will needed to film the scene from J's point of view, so the camera had to edge in beside his bent knee. But that proved a bad angle in regard to the door, catching Cate's face full on rather than in a flattering three-quarter view, and the purple blouse she had on did not work for the scene at all; it overwhelmed her expression. Three times they moved the mark on the floor she was instructed to walk up to when she entered the room. She changed into a pink blouse and then, when that didn't work either, a white one. The crew even considered abandoning the kneeling—too hard to shoot around—but Cate knew it was what her fans needed. J-lord played to them as rough and edgy. He had to seem romantic in a moment like this.

The "script" for this scene, written out by hand on a piece of paper and given to her ("You can improvise," Will said, though she did not) was as simple as it could be: a handful of "Oh my gods" and "it's so beautifuls"—with eyes on the ring—and one "yes, yes, I love you, yes." One "I want to be your wife, J." Cate had suspected they'd need reshoots. It was actually during the fourth take of the proposal that she had felt herself fill up with the sweetness of this change, the knowing that her future now had this certainty, of another human being in it.

This often happened with reshoots—on the third or fourth replay of something its impact became most real, her inner feelings ripened.

There were times, it was true, when Cate looked back at old episodes of the show and honestly could not tell you if a scene was reshot or if she looked at the original footage of whatever. There were no scenes they would categorically not reshoot—fights, sex, even the men in the show drinking too much and tossing blows, and in order to reshoot these scenes, J-lord, Andre and Alan had had to take acting classes to learn to throw fake punches and fall without hurting themselves. J-lord, being a performer, understood the need to do this, while Dre and Alan could get impatient.

Cate allowed her family a lot of leeway on how they appeared on the show, on what endorsements they would do. There was one thing the sisters wanted that she would not give them, however, and that was sex tapes of their own. Candy and Carlotta practically cried for this; even Cassie wanted one. Cate would not hear of it. Though these were private conversations, when Cate said no, Candy and Carlotta would get provoked enough to call her *psycho-bitch* and *control freak*, show phrases.

Each had plans, for how to shoot their video, how to fake the leaking of it, the tweets to sum up their indignation.

Cate's friend Riga, who had done well with her own sex tape, gave Cate the inspiration to make hers. The tape still existed, rentable on SeeTime for $14.99, an arrangement only possible because she and her sex partner signed consent forms. Still, she and the actor continued the pretense that the film had been private and stolen. The truth of her permission wasn't hard to figure out. It touched her, how her fans stubbornly accepted Cate's presentation of the world in spite of all evidence. Occasionally Cate had her sex partner Daniel fuel rumors her mother Cassie had leaked the tape. Fans loved that story. Daniel hosted a cable show about Hollywood back then, at the time of the tape, and wanted badly to act. Now he did action movies, tent-pole movies, big budget. The two of them still talked on the phone, had drinks: both of them seeing in the other the one who had been there when the spark of their real, present lives blew into flame, almost sharing a sibling relationship, a sibling knowledge of one another.

The tape showed the two of them taking a private plane to a resort in Mexico, a villa they had to themselves with a private pool. They both chipped in the money. You're selling a lifestyle, their director told them, not just screwing for an audience.

At Riga's advice, they had hired a porn director, a woman named Gina. Gina directed them through a variety of things, telling them when to make eye contact, when Dan should slap Cate's ass with a dull crack and set it seismically moving. Dan began by pouring water, slowly and sensually, across Cate's breasts and stomach, running it down through her trimmed pubic hair. Then Gina had Cate lie on her stomach while he penetrated her from the rear. Cate moaned *oh oh oh* in a kittenish voice while Dan said *You like this? You like this?* And she moaned *yes,* and *Oh shit shit I'm coming I'm going to explode all over you* and *Don't I make you happy?* every three minutes, whenever Gina held up a finger.

More orgasms would not be believable, said Gina, and fewer, disappointing.

It didn't matter what Dan did, Gina said, as long as his body showed, and he seemed in control. And it didn't matter what Cate did as long as her body showed and she seemed transported.

The description of the tape on SeeTime said *See Cate Crawley give everything,* and they meant of her body—mouth, ass, vagina, boobs—but

CC: Copy Cat

in a deeper way she had given everything; she looked into the camera and gave and gave. It was the last time she would look into the lens and wonder: Who might see it. What was next.

And though it had all been about male fantasy, it had led to women. It brought to her all the millions and millions of women who played her video game and bought her clothes and watched her show, though for these women, unlike for men, the sex would be obviously stagey, no real pleasure in it.

Cate sat at her computer, looking through a couple days' footage and making notes. It was the day of the Q meeting and the gym. She studied her face as it appeared on camera, an oval with large eyes and mouth and a slim nose, and thought of the vision of herself in the gym mirror, a face with so much more faceness to it—individual hairs in the brows, lines running down from the nose putting her faded mouth into parentheses, nose wider without its dark contour on the sides.

She saw with the usual tinge of bother the façade they used to stand in for the front of their real home; they never showed their house front, to keep away the fans (though oddly enough the façade was from a house right in the middle of Mulholland, and nobody ever bothered that family). The façade fronted a house of comparable size to the Crawley manse, but it had a fountain with a fake Greek statue—a handsome man with a slip of cloth around him, his left foot extended in front of his right, arms at his sides. The statue had a fountain spritzing up to it. Cate found the whole thing in poor taste. She had signed on to that house front when she had no real power with the network. Now, to change it, they would have to orchestrate a fake "move." It wasn't worth it.

As Cate back-buttoned and fast-forwarded, her eyes watered with the strain of focus, and she dabbed at them with a Kleenex, in the manner the Crawley women had developed for crying on camera: ball up the tissue, then poke upward at your eye, so as to keep eye makeup intact.

J-lord had gotten quite drunk recently, at a club of course, and cupped the ass of a waitress and punched out a paparazzo and smashed his camera. Cate studied the footage, thinking. None of this was unusual, but a young actress had been at the club, too, and slapped her hand against J's crotch while they were dancing. The actress, a monkey wrench of a being named Ciele, later tweeted that J "had quite the hard-on 4 moi, not w8ting for his Copy Cate Crawley." Now Cate had to decide whether to accept the offer of a feud and how to use it in social media and the show. Her younger fans would want her to take it on and throw back some smack talk. Her older fans found feuding tiresome.

Cate planned to edit the footage of J's night out at the club to imply that her own nagging and criticism of J, along with Cassie's sniping, drove him to drink and lech around. She found some footage of herself snapping at J for sleeping till the afternoon and made a note to weave it in with her mother telling him not to come shirtless to the dinner table. She scribbled out a sequence for the editor in which these two events would come in split screen, followed by a shot of J slamming a door behind him as he headed out for the night. In fact his club trip came days after both incidents, her mother had been kidding, and she and J had had a lovely dinner out that evening. The front door tended to slam itself.

"In love with myself," Cate said, quoting an article she'd read about herself that day. "Not hardly." She always edited the film to present herself as J-lord's downfall. She and Will edited all the film to make the C-Raws, including Cassie, seem awful much of the time. They screamed at each other, shoved and cursed. Cate could remember back to a time before the show, a time when house rules in the family precluded even *goddams*. Only occasionally did Cate throw in a trip to a children's hospital or a soup kitchen or something else altruistic. She actually did these things, but generally off camera. Cate had a deep understanding of how much of each type of behavior—good and bad—the fans wanted to see, though she could never explain herself well in meetings. What made people like you was hard, she thought, mysterious. Cate understood the proportions, but not the reasons.

If J had a downfall other than liking alcohol, it wasn't exactly Cate: it was simply that he knew a camera crew had orders to attach itself to him the minute he picked up a drink, or announced he was going off to a club, and stay with him as he got drunker and drunker. Otherwise J got little airtime. Sober, he was just not that interesting. Cate supposed she could be said, truthfully, to have led to his downfall, but not in the simple way viewers might think.

Cate had just fired a camera person for slipping J an Alcoholics Anonymous pamphlet. J was a magnificent drunk. He could scream curses at someone, his eyes glassed over and face red, turn his head to the side and stream vomit out of his mouth like a natural force, like a waterfall. He pulled his clothes off; he passed out, toppling straight down like a wind-whipped tree. He called Cassie an old whore and said things to Cate that ranged from mean, like *do you know how many girls would give anything to fuck me,* when she kicked him out of bed, to goofy, like *I bet we could make a beautiful baby right now, if it had your big ass you'd never push it out of you.* He slurred and babbled. The scenes were priceless and very hard to reshoot, though J was happy to try. He just turned into something else after four or more drinks, three-quarters of him a carousing who-gives-a-shit rock god, one quarter of him vaudeville buffoon.

But Cate had to face the fact that if the camera person had gotten worried enough about J to intervene, viewers would start feeling that way as well. The camera people were, in a way, their first, most focused viewers. And they were viewers, almost purely; they could only stop J from drunk driving, nothing else. They had to watch him fight, even if he got the worst of it, had to let him say things to famous performers and producers that damaged his career. The crew was the viewers' eyes, said Will. Eyes that couldn't shut, Cate added.

Funny, she thought; she got messages and mail telling her to stop J-lord from drinking, but nobody ever thought about the camera crew, following him even into the men's room to puke, into another woman's hotel room. No one took the knowledge that the show had to obtain permission to film in any public venue *before* setting up there to its logical conclusion.

Once again Cate needed to consider the question of rehab. A family intervention with J-lord would be dramatic. They would string out his agreeing to go into rehab over two, three, maybe even four episodes. He'd resist; there would be tears, pleas, ultimatums. Then the crew would shoot inside the facility—blurring patients' faces—and capture J in group therapy, also talking to counselors and doctors one-on-one. The sadnesses J kept inside—the mother who'd died two years ago of cervical cancer, his father the stunt man who laughed at J when he fell and cried as a child—would be released. New facets of J would appear. They would shoot family visits, conjugal visits with Cate, temptations thrown at him on release.

And then, after what? Six months, maybe? What would J's role be? They could film him prepping for concerts, in the family's usual sit-around-and-bicker shots. Squeezing the butts of Candy and Carlotta.

It wasn't much. The former scenes had become rote, the last could never lead anywhere. No one could survive on the show cheating with her sisters. She could forgive him; her viewers could not.

When Cate looked into her heart she found a steady secret warmth that was love for J. A sober J might be calmer but at the same time a sober J would lose the wild hold he had on the world's imagination. Cate had looked into the person J was and based on that, scripted a role for him that fulfilled all of what he wanted—and he loved her for it—but it might not be a role he could get away with playing forever.

Her love, in its way, was pure.

How long could he remain this J, she wondered. The happy sacrifice, mugging for the cameras. Not for always; he'd die that way. But until the end of the run of the show? Who knew when that would be? After five years their popularity had only increased. On the other hand, the Raw Girls were all now in their thirties.

Hard to know how long they'd remain appealing.

Cate asked her phone to remind her to call Martha tomorrow, the ghost poster who handled many of her tweets. She would take on Ciele but with just the right response—it would be reposted by the millions and had to be good. She would ask Martha for something sharp and witty but not angry—more along the lines of above it all, a shade patronizing. As if she really didn't care, which in fact, she didn't.

As she did when she closed out of the footage she reviewed, Cate slowed the video down and watched a little in real time. The black-manicured hand of Ciele patting the crotch of J's distressed jeans. Herself in the bedroom she and J shared, early afternoon, her hair wrapped around itself, and her calling the still-sleeping J a "slob-kebab." She had no idea where that phrase came from, but now her viewers would use it. Her brows made as if to knit together as she frowned at J, sprawled out across their bed, though they could not knit.

She imagined the millions of people who would watch all this, in a few days. Watch with love, boredom, jealousy, hatred, camaraderie, complicated feelings that took all these things and shook them together. It didn't matter. Eyes were like coins: they had an implicit value.

Cate had once taken a college course in linguistics. The professor had lectured about how in relatively short periods of time whole pronunciations, like of certain vowels and consonants, could change. One theory addressed why a whole class of vowels had transformed over a few hundred years, for reasons no one really understood.

"Some people think it might just have been a king with a lisp," the professor remarked. "One really popular king, or really scary king, same difference, and everybody tries to ape his speech. Then the right way to pronounce things just changes."

Cate thought back to this. She could do this, she realized. She would make a note to herself to do this, on the show. She would begin with the letter *S*. She would give a slight sh sound to her s's and soft c's—*trace, erase* to *trashe, erashe*, but very slight and subtle—and go out in public with no makeup on to mingle and see how it caught hold. She would be the modern king with the lisp.

Cate turned off the computer and walked up the curved marble stair and down the hall to her bedroom. She passed a column with a small Degas dancer, by a canvas with color swatches and a barely visible face, painted by Franz Ganz, an artist who believed thought itself was physical and could be seen and painted. *Oh God, if I had to worry about people seeing that too,* thought Cate, as she touched a finger to the flowing bars of paint. Maybe she kept the painting to remind herself of Ganz's error; within her head she enjoyed a blessed privacy. She fingered the Degas dancer and a Chinese vase. As she went to bed she always touched certain objects, her way of assuring herself of the things of her life, still existent for her in the real world.

J-lord had gone to bed early, and lay as he always did, his face scarved by an edge of blanket: just a muss in the covers, a log of humanity, snoring, with a whistle and a deep groan.

In the bathroom Cate pulled out wipes and removed the bright architecture of her face: her brows, her lips, the bronze and green on her lids and the black eyeliner on her upper and lower lids. She enjoyed the clean feeling of air on skin but somehow it bothered her too: this, and pulling the extensions out of her hair, unpeeling Spanx from her thighs. The loss of self, though having herself was a complicated owning. Her face, in the day, never seemed entirely hers. Her hair and makeup staff did her, so as much as she checked herself in the mirror and posted selfies from the makeup chair, when she was finished being done, there were surprises: not quite the mauve she expected on her lips, blue where she expected teal on the lids.

Cate's face was like a piece of theater, one of the audience participation kind, where people showed up, had input, and whoever came to the show—what makeup artists, what hair stylists and brow groomers—would change the performance wholly.

They brushed and coated and detailed her, often speaking as if she couldn't hear: "she's so fucking yellow," one said at Heidi's, and she didn't know if he meant her makeup, or her skin.

Cate could not, on her own, make herself who she was. This fact gave her an uneasiness and a prickly pride. Her beauty felt foreign to her in some ways, added on: in the same way she noticed at times, in her boobs and her ass, the implants that were in her but weren't her. Now, leaning over the sink to brush her teeth, she thought she felt the silicone globs move lightly in their own unsynchronized gravity.

It was a performance that could only exist for a time, with many people's participation. It being so provisional made her love herself more: in this moment of night, with its promise of morning and transformation in the glam room, the many photos and films she would take and others would take of her tomorrow that would record another day in which she had taken the challenge of being Cate Crawley, and pulled it off.

Someday of course time would march across her face with all the speed with which it had previously been held back.

She approached the bed, a custom-made king-and-a-half size, and slid into the sheets, 800-count and like silk. The bed was huge and lay like a boat or an ark against a cushioned wall. J-lord snored, four feet away, farther than he might be at a restaurant table. Cate had chosen to sleep nude tonight. It was late; the film crew gone. As she turned on her side the nubs of soft plastic settled themselves within her left ass cheek and her breast. She pictured them as islands of calm within her restless body, surrounded by nerves sparking, veins and arteries shooting blood. Cells splitting themselves and splitting more.

J-lord had once had a habit of wiping her makeup off. He did it on camera, back when he had high spirits. He'd say, *Cate, you look so much prettier without it*

J, you could never do what I do, she liked to tell him. She told her sisters that, and her mother, Cassie, who had an unwholesome drive to mimic her: her shoots for *Playboy* magazine, even her outfits, like a lace tuxedo she wore to the Grammys; the week after the Grammys Cassie wore the same outfit. Cassie tweeted Cate a photo. How she could smile like that at the camera, Cate wondered, knowing she was a copy?

Cate watched the planes of the blanket that would have been J-lord's face, had she revealed it. J slept sometimes with his shooting makeup on, contouring stripes on his cheeks, black liner smearing to black lid. His chest hair made spit curls here and there across his chest. Unlike the other men on the show, he didn't need to be depilated. He had thin and scattered body hair, no hair wads clumped on the breast area, no pubic arrow, as the depilators called the hair line from breast to crotch. It was a rare quality, in Cate's experience, with black-haired men. His sleeping face always looked childish. If she uncovered him, he'd look like a painted little boy.

Cate could wake him up and talk to him right now. She could tell him, *J, alcohol is going to kill you. You need to go to rehab, now. If you don't, you're off the show. That's it. I'll tell the camera crews you're poison. Not for a little while. Forever and ever.*

If she meant it—and he could tell—she would win. The drinking part of J's life would be over, easier to give up than this constantly being in front of peoples' eyes. That's what a regular wife would do, Cate thought. Not with the threat of withholding camera crews, but with something else essential, like sex, or seeing their children.

You can always count on me to be me, she told interviewers. The hair; the face; the body studded with islands of jellied rubber, these last parts independent of her, neither aging nor working against age. Though they would go down with her, like the buoyant lifeboats that nonetheless go down with the ship. Her answer was, she thought, the one true thing. Until, like Tita, there was no longer a true thing. She thought of her grandmother's eyes in their milky orbits, the rough pennies on her cheek. Then she turned over and went to sleep.

Fan: "Farewell, Good Ha Ha Ha"

Her mother took stabs at doing crossword puzzles, which she held in front of her as if the shape of her day lay within their blocks. Her mother also wondered where Fan was. She sat with crossword puzzles though her cognitive loss was so great she could not really be said to be doing them, and she wondered aloud where her daughter Frances was, now and in the past, though Frances sat with her in the small gold living room. She recognized Fan if her daughter was in her line of sight. The wondering about her seemed deeper than anything taking place at the present moment—though if Fan went to the bathroom or the kitchen the refrain would start: *Where's Frances? Wasn't Frances here?*

Her mother had used her Alzheimer's to accomplish the trick of editing her daughter out of her life, not the fact of her—she knew her daughter existed—but her physical presence. Her mother had always found Fan problematic for many reasons: gender, temperament, the timing of her arrival. Her daughter's black-haired, neat-featured good looks, drawn from her father's side of the family.

Her father's mother told her once, "You know, your ma is very jealous of you," and looked surprised when Fan began crying. "Oh, sugar, honey, it's not so rare," her grandmother said, and offered to read her a story. Fan was twelve years old.

Today her mother had been recalling a car trip they took when Fan and her brother were young. Once her mother came upon a shard of memory she would dwell on it. In this one the family drove to Missouri and back to see a set of grandparents. The drive took two days and on the return trip Fan caught flu, with a very high temperature; they crammed her brother in the front so she could lie stretched on the rear seat, with a blanket and a plastic beach pail for vomiting.

"Do you remember that trip to Creve Coeur, when Jack got so sick," she said to Fan's father. "We had to let him take off his seatbelt and sleep in the back coming home."

"Patty, that was Frances."

"You're right," said her mother, who was also hard of hearing. "Where was Frances? Why did we take a trip without Frances?"

"That was Franny, who was sick," her father said, and her mother eyed him doubtfully. A minute later she repeated her story and after a few corrections, her father gave up. He glanced at Fan, maybe wondering if she found him a traitor to her history. But even if her mother heard and believed what Fan's father said, she could not retain it, so within seconds the story would revert to its earlier form, with Jack.

Every day it seemed one memory, maybe two, captured her mother's imagination, but each focused on Jack, whether it had originally involved Jack or not. Her drawing Christmas cards with stick Santas and selling them in the third grade, though Jack would have found drawing girly at that age. Getting her front teeth chipped by a baseball at one of Jack's Little League games.

"Pats," her father said after the fifth or sixth repetition, "that was Franny. Why the hell would Jack have been in the stands at his own game?"

"You're right," said her mother, "that *is* funny."

Fan felt like a North Korean politician who'd been executed in disgrace and then stricken from the collective history.

Fan felt fairly sure—lacking wide experience in this area but just a long and concentrated one—that she did not love her mother the way most people loved theirs. She felt certain her mother did not love her in that expected way, either, but experienced Fan in her life as a strange shape, all knobs and angles, always in the way. Her mother, Patty or Patsy, came from a long line of women-hating women. She loved Jack, Fan's four-years-older brother, a child she found satisfying: male, introspective like her mother, a good student. Male.

She was a standoffish woman and was standoffish with Jack, but in a doting way. Patty's mother, Fan's other grandmother, used to say that all women hated one another. "If you got something, they want it, that's how women are made," she said with a hint of a brogue. Fan's mother said that women knew they couldn't do what men did so they could only compete with one another, for men and their attention.

Some women love women, Fan used to say. Her mother looked away.

Fan's father, whose name was Patrick and who was also confusingly known as Patty, recognized Fan's mother's flaws, though he also excused them.

"You know you can't blame your mother, Franny," he said. "Her generation, she was raised to think about girls a certain way."

Nevertheless her parents had many fights about her when she lived at home. Fan's mother refused to mother her daughter, making her care for herself, and she could be cruel to her, which got Fan's father upset. Fan lay in bed at night and heard them at it. Her mother said Fan *acted like she was the Queen of the May*, whatever that meant, and her father would scream, *Just cut her a break, Pats! Just cut her one break!*

Now Fan's father just worried about her mother, her Alzheimer's, the fact that she had broken a hip and walked poorly, needing a walker. He cried a lot—when Fan walked in the door, when she put out chicken and dumplings.

Fan flew straight to her parents' house from Korea. Hers had been older parents—forty-one when she was born—and now they were eighty-one. Both were in poor health, with her mother's Alzheimer's coming on top of diabetes, and her father having had heart attacks. Before her mother's Alzheimer's got bad, her mother did everything around their little house, from cooking to laundry to answering the telephone. Her father struggled with these chores and the two of them belonged in an assisted living place, but they wouldn't go. They didn't want to use Fan's (Paul's) money. She wanted them to, to quote King Lear's ambition for himself, *unburdened crawl toward death*. They chose the path of burdens, however. The Korea trip was the longest she'd been away from them in years.

She rested when she arrived at her parents' house, then pulled the gifts she'd brought them from Korea out of her suitcase. She shopped for them when she traveled, whatever she thought they might like: a silk scarf for her mother, a fan painted with girls in long dresses jumping on a seesaw. Place mats, cards. For her father, a letter opener, a calendar, a shirt. As usual she laid out her offerings and then as usual saw why they were all wrong: her mother, always cold, would wear no fabric but wool, and her eyes were too poor to make out the intricacies of the fan. Her father's busted-up hands couldn't manipulate the delicate letter-knife. When her mother saw the place mats she said, *They'll have to go to the dry cleaner's*, and Fan remembered that too would be a sticking point—one of her mother's Alzheimer's obsessions had to do with taking things to the dry cleaner's. Still, her mother passed the scarf along her neck and let the fan lie in her lap, only pushing the things aside at bedtime, less like she was enjoying them than like she couldn't imagine how to disengage; she sat like a Christmas tree with new ornaments hung on.

Fan asked her father to tell her about coal mining. She'd thought of this part of his life when in Korea, reading in the *Asia Times* about Chinese mine collapses. He told her about bootleg mines, holes in the ground the width of one man's body, dug by miners desperate for cash. These mines often began in hidden places and fed into regular coal seams. Miners would scrabble down into the ground, emerging with whatever coal they could chip off and sell it on the black market. Frequently the bootleg tunnels collapsed, crushing them.

"I went down two or three times," he told her. "You can't see your hand in front of you. You don't know if you're going to find a tunnel in front of you or a collapsed mess. You don't know if the guys waiting to pull you out are going to get chased off by the guards and leave you."

"Were you scared?"

"Hell, yeah. You just try not to let yourself think too much," her father, who Fan and her brother sometimes called Patty-the-Second, said. "You just get what you can and get out."

Greater than Fan's parents' need for her had been her need to get away from Paul. They'd spent three days in their apartment filling suitcases and then, as they (well, she) had bought a lot of stuff in Seoul, finding boxes and filling them too. These they would ship. But it got done. And it took her twenty-four ticking hours to ask Paul why they were leaving. In the meantime of frantic packing she flashed between thinking this was salvation and imagining Paul knew about Peter.

"Paul," she said finally, "What the hell's going on?"

He looked at her and she read in his eyes and mouth that their leaving had nothing to do with her. She saw this clearly, along with the fact that he dreaded this question and what it might hold even more than she did.

He breathed loud enough for her to hear.

"*Biologique*," he said. "They're retracting the paper."

At this point Paul was panting, something she had only heard him do during sex, an overlap that made the moment surreal and terrifying: his body so lost in all this.

"You don't understand," he said. He sat down on the edge of the bed, covered with the gaping mouths of boxes and suitcases. "They took it. We faked it."

"You did what?"

"We faked our data sets, our conclusions." Paul wiped his eyes against the cuff of his shirt. "We got to the stem cells but we could never get them to turn into anything, let alone neurons. It was In-Su. First we tried and tried to get the stem cells to go someplace, then we made these images and data sets. Eleven viable stem cell lines. They were brilliant, really. Elegantly done."

"You went along with this?"

Paul yanked on the cuff he'd rubbed over his eyes. "It seemed like the cells would learn to grow this way sooner or later, and this is what the data would have looked like." Then he reached into the suitcase next to him and grabbed her blue satin nightie, the one with lace along the neckline. He sat there twisting it between his hands.

"The magazine is running a piece on us, on the faking," he said, wringing and wringing her nightgown. "I can't get my name off the study but if I can get back to the States fast enough I can maybe pretend I didn't know."

She started to say, "Or what?" but of course she didn't need to be told. He would lose his job and never get another in his field, not if he applied to a high school. And if she'd ever known a man who could not do anything other than what he did, it was Paul.

Thinking back on this scene, from the relative calm—or ailing inertia—of her parents' house, Fan realized two things. One was that the thought of Paul in this situation, probably the worst thing that could happen in his career, had not made her think of the salary and the medical care, the comforts she would lose. She felt for him, in her heart, as if someone drove a screwdriver through her breastbone and turned it around and around in her chest. She understood why people said their *hearts bled* for things. Maybe it was an off heartbeat or valve fluctuation, but something physical loosened in her heart.

At his moment of confession, she placed her hand on Paul's head and then took it away.

Paul kept working her nightie between his hands and suddenly took it and slung it around his neck. She doubted he even realized he had it. But the gesture led to realization number two: he thought he would lose her over this. That thought, and not his job, made him suffer.

She considered for a minute and said, "Paul. I have to go from here to my parents' house, but that has nothing to do with you. Or what you did."

And she paid the transfer fee to get the airline ticket he'd purchased for her reissued, leaving Seoul two hours after she waved Paul through the security checkpoint at Incheon Airport, when she could feel how hard he worked for the small dignity of keeping his back, all the way through, turned away from her.

Fan had needed to visit her parents, but their house also formed a handy limbo. Deliberately she reset the terms of her life here: no Crawleys, no science reading. She wanted to forget the past months. She had never felt so much larger than Paul than she did at that last time together in Seoul, the dimensions of his world the size of her compact body. He called her several times a day while she stayed with her parents, cleaning or cooking or doing nothing at all, and she either didn't answer or got right off the phone. She'd get texts saying *are you there?* and she'd thumb back *yes* or *where else?* Paul had met with his department chair and his dean and told the version of the story he'd rehearsed with her: he had had only limited exposure to the lab in Korea, and once he knew In-Su had faked data he left, requesting his name be removed from the study. Unfortunately, and outside of his knowledge, In-Su had sent the false study, with his name still on, to *Biologique*.

The thought of the money, the comfort, crept in sometimes, but it lay over something deeper and less easy to articulate: she could imagine dealing with the individual pieces of the scandal, but she couldn't see how her life was ever going to make sense, to fit her, again. Paul would be fired. She could stay on, earning less than they needed to pay the most basic bills, as the wife of a disgraced professor. They'd have to sell the house. The garden she cared for, her moments of peace. The Paul would be so much with her.

Then again, she had betrayed him—in the most cynical way. Could this be her punishment? But they had both sinned. He'd wronged her, too, and let a lie *gross and palpable* into their relationship even before she had let hers in. Whose behavior had been more wrong, and on top of that, more ironic? It was hard to say.

Whether the chair and the dean believed Paul or not didn't matter. They would pretend they did, and then they would fire him if the scientific community did not absolve him. This was how their world worked.

Fan's mother continued to do the crossword puzzle every day. She could not think, so she handed Fan—her family had always passed crossword puzzles around—a puzzle blank but for answers that seemed random but weren't. She wrote *dry clean* in response to a fabric clue.

In a four-letter square with the clue "Times to remember" her mother filled in "dead."

And her mother had begun to sing. She sang in a falsetto Fan had never heard come out of her before. Her mother had a gruff voice but the sound coming out of her resembled the high thready voice of 60s singer Tiny Tim, and always the same words, as she clumped on her walker across the carpet: *I'm coming, I'm coming, though my head is bending low!* If she or her father or brother asked her mother if she was coming—to dinner, or TV, or to bed—she bowed her head and sang.

Fan's mother had never been pretty, but in old age she'd become other-worldly, bent and shrunk, and hunched over now at no more than four feet ten, thin, but with an oversized, almost triangular face, with large sharp features. She looked even older than her age, her angled body like a pocket knife half open.

"You look good," she said to Fan one day, rather accusingly. "I don't know why you look good." She touched her own head and added, "How have you kept your hair?"

Fan googled her mother's song one day: a spiritual, and the next line after the one her mother sang was, *I hear the angels singing. Gone from the earth to a better land I know!* It was a song about the moment of dying and about wanting to die, longing for that release. Though when she asked her mother, as she did several times, shouting till she was heard, why she sang that particular song, her mother had no idea why. Or she had an idea in one part of her head that the other parts couldn't find or interrogate.

"That silly thing," she answered. "Yeah, where did I pick that up from? I must have heard it somewhere. It must have been on the radio."

Fan thought about telling her father the lyrics but figured it would just upset him. In the original song, the word "though" was actually "for." In her mother's world salvation happened in spite of a bent head.

The last time she'd seen her mother, her mother made no sense: she babbled about how Fan had traveled to Latvia and woodcutters felled trees outside of the house. This new singing and the crossword puzzle answers, and the systematic blotting out of even Fan's childhood presence, felt like a betrayal, not just on her mother's part but on the world's. Her mother had faced down a mind melted into chaos and randomness, and transformed it into a kind of order, an order dictated by what she really valued in her inmost heart.

Her mother's cunning dementia felt Shakespearean. When Fan thought of her own time in Korea, the affair that had begun as daydreaming and then become incarnate, real as flesh itself and grotesque, mocked her. Her mother, a warped memory-less woman with a walker, had succeeded where she had failed, in reordering her life in accord with her imagination.

Fan's mother had always been averse to touch.

Now she needed help getting to the bathroom, getting dressed. Fan helped her wiggle into her Poise diapers as she sat at the edge of the bed, caught her slack sacks of breast into her bra and hooked it. Her mother, who had never gone beyond a peck on the cheek by way of affection with Fan, submitted to Fan's hands, even closed her eyes in enjoyment of a comb drawn slowly through her hair. Still, anyone could have done it. Fan was interchangeable.

At one point, during the down time between meals and cleaning up after meals, and while her mother napped and so needed no help going to the bathroom, Fan succumbed to an itch to write her stories down. But she had only chimera stories: one sort of start with a different middle and an unmatched end. And the harder she tried to pin her characters down the more they wiggled away from her: she realized she had no face for Mary/Marilyn/Molly or her counterpart; no hair style; no eye color. In what sense they had existed in her imagination she was no longer even sure.

Yoon began writing her. The first message from Yoon was a shock. Fan thought of her life in Korea as sunk into the earth, and now here was a dispatch from it in her email, subject line *Hello*. First Yoon simply wrote, *How are you?* in a message. Then Fan got a *where do you stay?* Yoon's messages were short: *I think about you, also me and my children.*

Fan pictured Yoon's lively, pretty face, in tears, no job or skills and In-Su sacked, with her young children. She seemed to be asking Fan, as delicately as she could, for help. Fan could not think of a thing she had to offer. She stopped writing back.

"Who's teaching your classes, Birdy?" her father asked her one day, a question that then became a refrain for her parents. "Birdy" was an old nickname (from her father saying of her, *eats like a bird*). Then her mother—through Fan and her father shouting it at her until she finally grasped the gist of the question—would chime in, "Yeah, who's teaching for you?"

"They assign you a substitute teacher?" her father asked.

"Not in college they don't, no," Fan said. "They just reassign classes to other teachers." He looked unsatisfied.

"They have enough teachers so they can do that? Or do they just give everybody more students?"

"In college they don't have to offer all the same classes all the time," Fan said, adding, "It's complicated."

Her mother, having asked a question, could be counted on to repeat it several dozen more times, so Fan found herself giving a long answer the first time her mother asked who took over her classes, then shortening it and shortening it till she just said, "no one."

"No one!" said her mother, wonderingly.

She had spent three weeks at her parents'. They'd scheduled in their doctor's and dentists' appointments while she was there to drive and help them, and she had cooked and frozen meals, loading up the appliance her mother called an *icebox* and her father called a *Frigidaire*. She went out for the odds and ends they needed: a mop, a new clock, a digital scale. Plumbers had been called for a slow toilet. She had washed the window by the spot on the couch where her mother sat, going in slow circles from a cross of Windex. She and her father tried to watch musicals on TV, like *Chicago* and *A Chorus Line*—her father loved song and dance—but her mother snapped, *Why aren't those women wearing anything? Turn it off!* and Fan's father did.

Fan told her father they had returned from Korea early and she could stay a while, but he had begun asking her about Paul, first saying

Fan: "Farewell, Good Ha Ha Ha"

How is Paul managing without you? Then, *Everything alright between you two?*

"Fine, good," she said. "Paul's really busy. And I haven't seen you guys in a while."

In her head she pretended there was no such thing as time, as Einstein taught. "For those of us who believe in physics," Einstein wrote to a friend's widow, "the distinction between past, present and future is only a stubbornly persistent illusion." Fan loved the way Einstein listed physics as a belief among beliefs—it could have been a belief in apocalypse or Christian Science—so she too could believe.

Without time she would have nothing to worry about: not the impossible new life, not how work would be in the future, taking one step after another in a slog of shame. She thought of those bootleg miners and how they must have practiced the same discipline: timelessness meant no shifts in the earth's crust, no seismic heaves, no clutch of mineral pressing the life out of them.

Her father was not privy to Fan's inner stop-clock, though, and he began counting off the days to her: "It's been two weeks now Franny," "twenty days on Sunday." Her mother when Fan left the room now said, *Where's Frances? Frances is at the airport, isn't she?*

Her daily indulgence was a bath. She poured into the running water a cap full of bubble bath that smelled like grape gum, from a purple bottle she'd had since childhood. But the chewing gum odor and the sight of her skin trying to slough at the surface but staying put, flaky and dry, put her in a complex nostalgia. Her mother's angular body, weak though it was, reminded her of the ddemiri and the geometry of muscles always in argument with the black bikini. She wanted to be back at the jjimjilbang, and she still had the bikini top, wearing it under her clothes. She imagined staying at Dragon Hill—travelers would check in and stay for days at a time, as it was cheap—and living her life going from pool to pool, clock-free, from peeled skin to risen drench.

She could call Paul and ask him to move out, then return to their house for some alone time. She couldn't go back to her job until the new academic year started at the end of August, though, meaning she'd have to ask Paul to give her money. She tried calculating on a piece of paper how much she would need to last till then, just making the mortgage payment and utilities, and spending the minimum on food, and came up with an impossible sum. She could send out dozens of letters offering her services as adjunct faculty to other universities and get ready for the epic silence that would follow.

She sat with her mother one afternoon. Her father had gone off to shower.

"Tell me where is fancy bred," her mother said suddenly, not looking at Fan but staring into space. Her eyes looked gleamy. "How begot, how nourishèd? Reply, reply."

A song from *The Merchant of Venice*. But that made no sense; her mother did not know Shakespeare.

"Mom. Mom? What are you saying?"

Her mother gave her an angular grin. "It's the Bard." She went on, "Of course they didn't mean fancy the way we mean fancy. Not like, you know, fancy clothes."

Fan said, "Oh," lamely. It was unlikely at any given time that her mother could hear her unless she shouted; women's voices, due to pitch, were hardest to hear of all. Her mother spoke at her, or at something or someone she imagined in the room.

"My daughter likes that Shakespeare," Fan's mother said, speaking to the air again. "She wrote something about him once. How there was two of everything, or something like that."

"That was Kyd, Mom. My dissertation. Doubling in Thomas Kyd," said Fan, a little desperate, but her mother didn't look at her. She picked up her Korean fan and began fanning herself, hugging her sweater close around her, as if she were making herself cold.

Fan's father stood at the door of the room in his plaid bathrobe. "She's on that Shakespeare thing again, huh," he said. "She's been doing that. I don't know where she's getting it."

Fan felt, with the sensation of a chisel to the brain, that what lay in her head was no longer her own. Even her mother, who had no use for her, had tapped in. It felt like she spilled out of herself; it felt like falling. And as she tumbled she could see herself from the outside, a woman lucky to be who she was, pretty with a fine nose and black eyes, privileged to have enough (how many people throughout history, born in her proximity to poverty, would have enough?), privileged to be well and warm.

Fan saw the man with the broken leg in Korea, the other one with Styrofoam shoes, both men she had never given anything but the gaudy butterfly of her attention; Yoon who had tried so hard for her; the ddemiri she had stolen from; Peter and the woman or women who probably lived on the other side of his story; her mother who wished her out of being but still allowed Fan to decorate her with useless things; her father and his pride and his tears; Paul. She'd seen them with so little need that she could watch them as if they lived to perform in front of her. She came to her life as an audience, a petted, cranky audience, sitting on her hands.

She called Paul. She had not called him in more than a week.

"I'm online looking for a ticket," she said, though she wasn't, yet. "No later than Friday." It was Wednesday.

He only breathed for a minute. "You're coming back."

"Yes."

"It's OK then."

"I guess so. Yes."

"The retraction's done," he said. "*Biologique.* They took my name off the paper. I'm not mentioned in it." Paul didn't appear able to talk in more than short bursts.

"Oh?" She had not expected this.

"Turns out my dean knows the editor. I think she may have made a call, pulled some strings."

"So your job?"

"I still don't know. They may want me discreetly gone."

"We'll manage," she told him. "I'll forward you my reservations."

"I'll get you at the airport. Please don't hang up."

"OK," said Fan, though she hadn't really talked to Paul in so long she felt a little at a loss for words. "How's the garden?"

"The crocuses are up in the front. And something else. Little blue flowers along a stalk."

"Are you outside?"

"Yes."

"Those are the hyacinths." And she had him take the phone and walk his way around the beds. He stopped frequently and said, "I don't think the so-and-so is coming back," about the peonies and geraniums, and even about the voodoo lily, a plant that had an eight-inch purple-black spadex, a swollen phallic thing that bloomed for a few days once a year and reeked of decay. The spadex drew flies, which pollinated it. She had planted the voodoo lily for Paul, for its cloning-type grotesquerie.

She said of the peonies and the geraniums, "They're just not up yet," and of the voodoo lily, "Do you see anything growing where it was? A stake that looks like sharpened bamboo? Like, you'd hide it with grass and use it to impale your enemies?"

Silence as Paul leaned over. "Yeah. About a foot high? Terrifying."

"That's it," she said. "It will all be back, don't worry."

PART III

Fan: What Comfort to This Great Decay May Come

Fan flew home and she and Paul slipped back into one another. Fan: as if Paul were a bed, rumpled and easy and deeply imprinted with her body. Paul: as if she were clothes, stiff, nicer than he felt he deserved, all that stood between him and existence pounding on bare skin.

They discussed nothing at first. Or, none of what they needed to. Fan's confession about Peter would be more hurtful; Paul's story about his faking and his job more life-divisive. They had a gift for banter that could take them through days and days of circling around the rest, each of them aware of the circling. They talked about voodoo lilies and her mother's crosswords and dinner.

"Guess who was taking orders at the Piehole and said she'd deliver? Gwen," Paul said, of the owner of their upscale pizzeria. Fan turned to him, diverted, as Paul had known she would be. Gwen hated actually working.

"Gwen taking orders. Business must be off," she said, her mind wandering to Gwen, her freckled face and long pale hair. When Gwen worked the register, which she did occasionally, she did it bouncing lightly on a giant exercise ball. The ball was blue. As Fan explained she wanted ranch on her salad, Gwen smiled her loose contented smile and repeated everything back ("Baby greens. Ranch.") and bounced. Gwen tended to call her own actions *modeling self-care and positivity*—that was how Gwen talked—and Gwen's ball-bouncing self-love made Fan wild with irritation. Was Fan irked enough by Gwen to be secretly glad if her business was off? Sadly, she was, and her epiphany about herself at her parents' house hadn't lasted very long.

"I'll get the door," said Fan. And when the bell rang and she got their order—the Mad Greek pie, with feta—Gwen took her money with that loose smile and an infuriating *Blessed be*, as she palmed the tip.

Fan pulled the door shut. "Blessed be? What in the holy hell is 'blessed be?' Blessed be who exactly? Victor?"

"It's Wiccan, babe."

Paul in their early marriage would be the kind of husband who asked, Why don't you just find another pizzeria if she bugs you so much? Now he was the kind of husband who helped out, tickling just enough her sensitive irritations.

Fan took to wearing her hair in a bun. And she felt loose-ended still. May came, following what felt to Fan like a swift April, though she'd done little. Paul had been put on paid leave, she was not teaching yet. She downloaded samples of several dozen new novels she felt she should read, scanned the pages and then decided she didn't want to read them. Each seemed to promise a life in which dramatic, meaningful (if tragic) things happened—a couple who'd desired one another had sex, then the woman fell asleep in her car on a highway and died; a man fell in love with his wife's brother, who got killed suddenly in a sudden war.

People turned out to be one another's children, or secret lovers. Deaths happened out of the blue. The inward, melancholic woman had long ago given up her lovechild for adoption, and so she became inward and melancholic. It was a secret revealed at the end. Characters suffered, had thoughts about suffering, then information emerged that explained them. When they died they died in interesting ways. Lives, Fan had decided, were like clones, with most warped, bulbous and out of kilter. Out of hundreds came the one that worked as art. Fiction took only that one somehow proportionate life: it might not be a good life, but it looked like something from a distance.

Maybe everything looked like something from a distance, Fan thought, but we don't live at that distance. We live up close.

Paul urged Fan once or twice to try fiction again and each time she explained herself—about real life, the scarcity of reasons for anything— and he didn't understand.

"So you leave those parts out, you write the interesting stuff," he said.

"Those parts are what there is," she said, and added, "It would be like doing what you did with your data sets," which was unkind, but it annoyed her that he found her discipline to have less of a truth ethic than his own.

Fan's father had been hungry as a child, his family once living for a week on raisins and cheese. He said to her, *It was that, as much as the mines, that made me run.* They didn't have enough cheese and so he ate raisins, woke up to them, chewed more at bedtime to quiet his stomach. It marked him: he could never look at a raisin again, and they were forbidden in Fan's home. Fan had been punished more than once for bringing home a raisin-studded cookie.

When he ran away from home, her father said, he pictured running to a place like something he'd heard about, a place with a refrigerator that you opened and its cold exhale breathed out of shelves and shelves of food.

"I hardly even noticed I was wet, hardly noticed I was working," he told her once of the Merchant Marine. "All I knew was, I went into that mess hall, I could have as much of everything as I wanted."

Fan knew that if you lost the people around you, if you lived in violent circumstances, much of your life would be grieving. But even with poverty or hunger or grief marking your life, life would stay messy and inconclusive. Her father's story mattered—hunger mattered—but how would you tell it, what would be the end point? Fan remembered her fiction classes and the inverted check mark she'd been taught, the conflict-crisis-resolution shape of the story or the novel. In fact we don't have sharp peaks of action like that, good or bad, just bumps that bump you along the road.

Because even a dream like enough food would come to seem ordinary if you achieved it. Her father evolved into a man who could stand in front of the fridge, sigh and say, *There is nothing to eat*, though her mother had always kept it full. He'd lost that joy in abundance and just kept the loathing, of a tiny wrinkled fruit. And that story was the story. Not one anyone wanted to read.

Each morning Fan sat in her garden picking roly-polies out of her strawberry patch. The bugs had taken to mawing a hole in each ripe berry. She tweezed the roly-polies off the ground and dropped them into her cupped palm, where they curled their plated backs into a bead, a steely bead like punk jewelry. Often she found herself stopped, tweezer in her right hand, staring at the live legged crawlers stilled into rounds. She thought of stringing them into a necklace, making a video of herself stringing and wearing it, going viral on the internet. The insect jewelry woman. Her roly-poly rosary. How long would the insects stay curled? They seemed capable of staying that way forever.

Fan's FOMO was kicking up, though she rarely posted anything. She mentioned the viral roly-poly jewelry thought to Paul, who said, Do it! Make a necklace.

But then she'd think about the watchers who'd condemn her for harming bugs, question how she could think of doing this silly thing when X was going on in the world. That kind of fame burned soon into condemnation. That world was like academia, which could never love an idea for very long.

Paul would catch her ruminating, kneeling over strawberries.

"Why don't you just poison the damn things?" he said of the roly-polies, which he called *pillbugs*. "You know, you could use something safe, like neem oil, or Bt."

"They're crustaceans," she said, "you can't kill them. They breathe through gills. They've got this shell." She waved her beaded palm under his eyes. "*Armidilliididae*. Like armadillo. Like armored."

"Arma-silly-dildo-dates?" She laughed and he added, "There must be something you could use."

"Nothing you'd want on your food."

Fan kept tweezing the bugs, and elsewhere planted wild strawberries, which she ordered online and which arrived in a box, stems thin as a hair, tucked into dirt. As she worked, she thought about what she needed to say about Peter. *You left me,* she could say, with some honesty, *not physically, but mentally, and mostly you were never there physically either.* She could say, *I regretted it before it even happened,* and *it wasn't pleasure, it wasn't like it is with you.* All these things would be true, but with that pruned truth she found in novels.

Finally Paul offered her a small truth and without really meaning to she offered him a large one. They had just eaten. Paul grilled bulgogi, Fan opened a jar of farmer's market kimchi, foods they'd missed from Korea. They drank rose, in their outdoor way: jelly jars filled very high, then nursed.

"No wine works well with sesame oil," said Paul, and abruptly, "There was a moment when we had our article and our data ready to go out and it was just so beautiful. I thought when the time came I'd have to tell In-Su I couldn't do it, but then I just wanted to. I wanted people to see it. I imagined *Biologique* and then newspapers and my name all over this cool elegant thing. Like when people see me with you."

Fan said, "Weren't you a little scared?"

"Not at that moment. You couldn't doubt something like that."

"What was beautiful about it?"

"The phase contrast imaging, the pluripotency markers. The DNA fingerprinting analysis—it all had just the right amount of right to it. He put in the perfect amount of failure. His failures were genius, actually." Paul absently tugged at his eyebrows, pulling the hairs straight out. The longest was more than an inch. "When I *read* it all I believed it. Like a great novel, like that feeling it should have happened and so it would. Then I thought, let's just get the publication and the resources and it'll happen after."

"Did you know about the women?"

Fan had read the retraction about to appear in *Biologique*, sent by the magazine's editors to the authors. The hoax had been exposed in Korea, by another researcher who demanded to see all eleven stem cell lines the men claimed to produce. After a lot of delaying In-Su sent him some samples. Analyzing these, the researcher realized all had come from a single cell line and lacked pluripotency, the ability to turn into anything else. In addition to reporting this, *Biologique* reported In-Su had paid some women several thousand dollars to harvest their eggs. This kind of payment was strictly forbidden in Korea.

"I didn't," said Paul. "No. I swear. Not a hint about that." He wiped a finger around his mouth guiltily. He seemed to think Fan would find this fault particularly egregious, though she didn't. She was, mostly, curious. How did you decide what to pay women for their eggs? How did you have that first conversation about it?

Fan rose and went to her strawberry patch, gathering them berries—intact ones, the roly-polies' numbers finally diminishing. She put some in Paul's jelly jar and some in her own. "Sorta Sangria," she said.

"Sortagria." He drank, rolling a berry around in his mouth.

"Do you remember my Korean class? Do you remember Peter?"

His face, when he looked up at her, had curled inward, and she saw in that an image of every live thing's self-protection.

The way she put it was: *We had an afternoon, a sarang bang.* And then she heard the unintentional pun. And thought: Oh God, Paul could never miss that either.

In the end it worked because things work when they have no choice beyond working. Paul went through both anger and shame. He sat silent, jammed his thumbs together without moving them or watching them, glared at her as if to say, *Even this consolation you've robbed from me.* He also said over and over, "I knew I was ignoring you." She told him that it wasn't that, exactly, he'd been busy before, but she couldn't quite describe his jazzy manic energy, the way it seemed to absorb her and obliterate her. And the strange insight on the ferry: the production line of Fans. Trying and trying to get back to her, as he convinced himself she was in some way repeatable.

She said, "You stopped seeing me," which held a bit of the truth. She realized now that if he had allowed himself to see her, he would have felt the need to confide in her. And as she lost his eyes on her, Peter's eyes on her became important. Perhaps it was all that simple.

She said to him, "It helped me realize you're everything to me," which again had truth but parsed it.

For a few weeks Paul stayed mostly silent, took walks, went out with his laptop and stayed out. He came home smelling of coffee and hot milk. They talked about minutiae as always, but less, and often when they sat in the same room, it was silent, so silent Fan didn't know what to do with her hands. She pressed them between her thighs, feeling like she'd never noticed them before. Then a small package came to Paul in the mail, shipped overnight, and he opened it and without a word handed her a necklace of metal beads, plated around, exactly like curled up roly-poly bugs.

She put it around her neck and it reached right to where her heart lay thumping inside her chest: she'd wondered irrationally, when she saw the package, if he was handing her divorce papers. A few times the beads tapped against her heart, which felt like a hamster trapped in the bars of her ribs. The beads she found quite ugly.

"Thank you," she said, "it's perfect," and they stood there, both aware they had rowed together against a dismal wave topped up to drown them, and now pulled their boat out of the water.

Paul's dean, to both of their surprise, hoisted his other stricken vessel onto land. Of course, the dean did this for herself and the school's reputation, not for him, but her motives hardly mattered. When the dean emailed Paul and Paul's department chair Dwight about a meeting in her office, Paul clutched Fan's wrist in terror. Without his beard, his face looked open, transparent, and she could see the agitation of his cheeks.

Paul's panic reminded Fan of his strange breathing when he told her the story of the faking, back in Seoul. Paul assumed the dean had called him in to fire him. In fact, she wanted to tell Paul she'd gotten him signed on to a cloning team at an institute in Scotland, one of the teams that had worked on the cloning of Dolly the sheep. To Paul's shock, this team had arrived at the verge of creating viable pluripotent stem cell lines, histocompatible with the donors, what he and In-Su pretended to do. Paul would join the team and his name would be one on the paper announcing this news. *Biologique* would run an item about his joining the group, with a note saying his part of the In-Su research had been real, groundbreaking, and now he took his expertise to a place where it could be used in a valid and ethical experiment. He was personally shocked, shocked and hurt, at how his research had been misused.

The dean, a woman named Pfleuger, stared Paul down and told him all this with a loud but neutral recitation, as if, Paul told Fan later, she recited the script of a television movie to someone a little deaf. Fan had met Pfleuger once. The dean wore her hair in a bun covered with a gauzy veil, and had earrings shaped like two little hammers. She hunted. Dead animals, some horned and quite large, rested at odd angles in framed photos throughout her office. Most had a Pfleuger limb couched on them somewhere, the dean posing. She snapped at Fan, when Paul introduced her, "Why does your department call itself English? Mathematics doesn't call itself Number!" Everyone called her Battleship Pfleuger.

Anyway, Battleship Pfleuger turned her prow toward the problem and sank it, water closing around seamlessly. In-Su had been badly disgraced—fired, and the subject of newspaper stories, leads, one after another. His success had been national news in Korea; his failure was proportionally so. It did not suit Pflueger to deal with notoriety in one of her faculty. She had, it turned out, her own channels. Before any official announcements about the Scotland move, Paul started getting emails from peers in his field, all of whom had been long silent. I'm sorry, they said, how unprofessional of In-Su to involve you. Dude, said one of the hipper ones, uncool. Glad you're in the clear.

Smart of you, wrote another, to keep your own lab, the way things turned out.

Paul understood that a narrative of his recent days circulated, one he had little knowledge of. He kept Fan up on the rumors of who he was that reached his ears. He never, he told her, disagreed with anyone now, even those far removed from cloning, even a colleague one day remarking that Paul's office was blue.

"Who knows these days but that it is blue," he said.

"Pflueger blue," said Fan.

"And wouldn't that be a paint chip," said Paul.

Paul headed off to Edinburgh for all of July and August. Dwight told Paul that part of the deal would be the Institute "running him ragged," and Fan used this as an excuse not to go. She also began teaching in August. And the Peter confession had put so many subjects off limits between the two of them: whether others thought she was pretty, whether a dress or a pair of earrings looked good on her, men in general, even whether Paul thought she was pretty. And Korea and all things related to Korea. As a result they talked about very little but the one crisis they could talk about, the cloning. Paul met with Pflueger in mid-June. By then Fan felt she couldn't take it anymore, the "NT hESCs" that sounded so much like "empty nests," the histocompatibilities, this or that data set, the *Korea Times*. Every day felt like a steaming bath in Paul's misery. She wanted to live for herself for a while.

So she found herself at home, in a situation reminiscent of Korea, doing whatever might catch her imagination. She would think *whatever I fancy* and then stare out the window thinking about the word *fancy* in that usage. It was a contraction of *fantasy*, a version of the word that came to be used when the thing you fantasied had an element of choice. You could do it, if you fantasied it.

Paul called nightly from Edinburgh, where, he said, his hotel room had a tartan spread and a poster describing the family the tartan belonged to (the McDavids—apparently, Paul told her, they disliked feudalism but had a great passion for sheep). The hotel put out cheap sherry in a crystal decanter every night at six in the drawing room (Mogen David meets cooking wine, was how Paul described it), and had a ceramic haggis on a table in the same drawing room, with, of course, Robert Burns's haggis poem.

"And a haggis is?" Fan asked, though she knew.

"A gut filled with more guts, and some oatmeal," said Paul.

"That's nice, it's like breakfast and evisceration, all at once."

Fan asked how the lab seemed. She meant whether he felt like they knew the real story, if he carried a whiff of disgrace into work with him. He understood her, and said they seemed to respect and think well of him.

"And I know more than I thought I did," Paul said. "In-Su cheated, but his ideas were sound. He was smart."

"That's great," said Fan, "that's really great," with many things moving in her head: whether Paul would actually find his perfect life without her, *his* fancy, but that thought perched beside gratitude that he was fine, that she could stay at home, making a life for herself that felt wholly created, from the blastocyst onward.

"Pay attention to the maids, Paul," was all she said. "Remember to tip," and he said, *you call me that now*, meaning Paul.

"Why not. It is your name."

Fan weeded her garden, ate frozen foods from an upscale grocery, foods she'd always wondered about: plantain empanadas, Australian hand pies. Foods that had intricate descriptions and beautiful package photos and cost eight dollars a box, though the items always turned out to be wizened and bland. Fan was a curious eater. She wanted to try what looked interesting, even if she guessed she'd be disappointed. Paul had categories he would have none of, like frozen food. And it really wasn't very good, so she took to cooking simple meals of pasta or fresh udon. Tomato sauce, soy sauce, gochu jang, Parmesan, kimchi: she boiled noodles till slippery, then heaped on some combination of these flavors. She ate salads and chalky protein powder mixed with hemp milk, balanced with chocolate. For a while she ate candy bars from her childhood every night—Kit-Kats, Mounds bars, Reese's Cups—then she lost interest. She bought the best chocolate she could get and kept it on top of the refrigerator, breaking off squares to eat whenever she walked by.

Her yard had a water sculpture she enjoyed sitting by, in the evenings, hearing and seeing the water cascade over a round stone and down the sides of a rectangular one. The water sculpture was new, and the neighbor's cat would wander over and flick her paw at the water, trying to catch it, while she sat outside with a glass of Sauvignon Blanc or a Guinness or a Korean sijo.

In Korea Fan had downloaded the Crawley video game on her phone. It was called *Crawling Up the Ladder* and in it, you played an "E-lister," someone not famous, who had to become an "A-lister" by dating celebrity men, acquiring designer clothes, and getting photographed in chic places. You had an avatar, a curvy cartoon that represented you, and the avatar had to glam up, and then you would get admitted to the clubs and parties where you might get dates.

The game only let you date men, though influential female friends could get you points. This retro sexuality bothered Fan, but, she told herself, it was a game, just something to pass the time. She got the game free but had to buy "Crawley Cash" with real money in order to work on her look—whether through buying clothes and accessories or hiring hair and makeup artists.

The C-Raw women popped up as you played to give you advice and invite you to events, but you could only attend if you had the right face and clothing.

She'd stopped playing the game during Paul's troubles. Now it urged her back, her phone pinging with messages the game sent, the first threatening to knock her off even the E list. When she ignored that, a headline rose from a fake gossip magazine called *Star Turns*: "Who's talking about Francesca lately? Uh, yeah, us neither." Francesca was the name of her avatar in the game, a girl who looked like Veronica from *Archie*, but with bigger boobs.

The notifications started to feel a little creepy. Fan had entered the game through Facebook and she imagined it might start posting nasty things about her game-self there—the E list loser with no media attention.

Fan talked back to her phone, telling it threats wouldn't win her back. Then, guiltily, she started playing again. Her Francesca walked down Hollywood Boulevard. She passed a mansion and a door that had previously had a lock icon now had an arrow, meaning she could go in. She entered, and as Fan swiped her finger around the phone her other self mingled at the party. A barrel-chested man with a balloon identifying him as a stunt double named Dirk Dillard asked her to go to a place called D'Andrea's with him. The game burbled and made a clapping noise.

A text box opened saying, *Congratulations E-Lister, you have a date with a D-Lister! Now get your date noticed in the media!*

Fan was absurdly delighted. When Paul called later, asking what was new, she almost squealed that she had a date. The game: really a terrific piece of salesmanship. A video game promising to rise you to the level of anyone else famous, a naturally beautiful, talented, singer or actress, would be hollow. Being a Crawley—an invented face, no vocation but in living itself—was a fantasy you could fancy.

This life—the game, the candy, the food that felt like answers to mild but long overdue questions—was precious but it didn't last. Jack her brother called. Early July, the day after the Fourth, a day for her of wine in the yard and distant fireworks.

He said, "Franny." He never called her this; he called her Flass or Flassy, an old, lispy nickname. And they had a way of talking to each other, a commiserating voice they fell into: I've been hanging out with Pop, you know he's Pop, Jack would begin: he thinks we should have had children, he's counting off on his fingers his friends with kids in high school. They take shop classes and make their grandfathers wooden pig cutting boards. This is *heav*en, apparently.

Wooden pig cutting boards, Fan would say, I'd get him one of those.

It's not the cutting board itself, that's a mere bag of shells, said Jack, voicing one of their father's pet phrases. Next they'd get into their mother. Now, though, Jack sounded brusque and formal, like a newscaster.

"Mom's in the hospital. First she had a urinary tract infection, and it hasn't gotten better, and now God knows what. She's blind in one eye and her face is sagging."

"A stroke."

"They're saying not," said Jack, "but nobody seems to know really."

"What are they doing? When's she getting out?"

"No idea. They can't figure out what's wrong. She's stopped eating. And," Jack used this word as if he were choosing it from a list of the most neutral terms he could think of, "she's agitated."

"Agitated? How? She's in St. Jude Over Water?" Fan remembered how people nicknamed their local hospital *St. Jude Undertaker.* "I'll get right there."

"It's hard to describe how she is, you just have to see. And for coming now, I don't know," said Jack, and Fan realized that his voice reflected exhaustion, and probably their father's nearness. "It might be better to wait till Friday. Friday I have to go." Friday was three days away.

"But it might be over by then," Fan said, hoping Jack would illuminate her as to what "over" meant in this case: her mother better? Or dead? She couldn't tell what outcomes they were dealing with. And Jack answered, "It's not going to be anywhere near over, I don't think."

She tapped through the over-lit corridors of St. Jude's, so refrigerator-white she half expected that cold exhale and the odor of meat and old fruit. Took the massive elevator with doors that opened on different sides depending on the floor, so she'd fallen out once as the door she leaned on slid. Photos of the recent Popes lined the wall, the men in the miters that looked like a golden napkin folded on a restaurant plate. A crucifix here and there, a niched Mary. Fan had made the four-hour drive on an empty highway. Now she faced the opposite—searching for her mother's room, on the neurology wing, a stream of people went the other way down the hall, doctors and nurses in green scrubs, patients pushing their IVs on footed stand. Visitors, in old jeans or business suits, grim or tired or tearful, or even jolly.

She found the room and turned into it, thinking of her brother's word *agitated*, the sense of a list, a pull-down menu of words he could have chosen.

She got right away why Jack had had to think. A rabid animal had clawed its way into her mother's body. That was clear enough, if hard to articulate.

Her mother's skin had split somehow and the creature leaped in, trapped and kicking its way out. A lynx or an ocelot, a wolf. Patty's was an inhabited body, a sacrifice to some animal god. She tossed, rose and flailed, all her limbs working out from the pale, six-inch-wide belt tied around her waist and buckled around the hospital bed. Tiny as she was, the belt swallowed her torso, a still point around which she lurched and lashed.

FAN: WHAT COMFORT TO THIS GREAT DECAY MAY COME

Fan went up to her and took her mother's hand. Her mother stilled, then scratched her, deeply, wet red lines along the palm.

"Fran," said her mother. So her mother knew her; Jack had said she recognized him and their father, no one else so far. She'd forgotten her siblings, not just what they looked like but that they existed. Fan's Aunt Glo came to sit with her sister-in-law; her mother didn't recognize her either. Here she was, though, Fan real in her eyes.

"Take me home, Frances. They're not very nice to me here." Her mother's seeing eye squinted and searched Fan's face. The right eye rolled milkily the other way. Her mother clutched Fan's hand, looked with a stern air of wonder. "I just came here to visit somebody. Who did I want to visit? But now they won't let me leave."

"You're sick, Mom, you can come home when you're better," Fan said, but realized her mother's hearing aids were out. Suddenly her mother began flailing again, and she shrieked. In her shriek the weird falsetto of her singing had changed to something ghastly, ululating through the room and out the door and down the corridor. *Take me hooooome! Take me hooooooooome!*

The corridor traffic—the green-clad people, visitors, the IV patients—slowed down, looked.

A nurse appeared, an older woman with a cloud of permed, orange-soda hair. "Are you the daughter?" she asked. "I told your father we're going to have to put her on a course of Haldol if we can't get her quiet."

"Haldol's an anti-psychotic," said Fan.

"Exactly," said the nurse. She stared at Fan in a way that reminded her of Pflueger. "She scratched my orderlies and took a swing at one of my LPNs." Fan felt like a mother hearing her kid's been fighting at preschool. Humiliating, but how the nurse felt she could have stopped this she didn't know.

"You've got her tied down."

"You've seen her. Smacking at everything, trying to jump. She'd break every bone in her body."

"Well," Fan said lamely, "I just got here."

"She thought your father wanted to let her die so he could marry my nurse." Once again she eyed Fan as if Fan had written the script for this, and could change it if she wanted to.

"Where is my father?"

The nurse waved down the long white corridor. "There's a caretaker's room. He's been staying in there. He can't take much more either, from that one." She bobbed her head at Fan's mother and displayed a little cup. "I'm giving her a pill now." She stared at Fan again, as if daring her to stop her.

Of course Fan's father Patrick cried when she found him. He bent his face into the bowl of his hands, and tears slid between his fingers. That seemed like far more water than should come out of you. She gripped his shoulder.

"They're giving her some medicine, Pop. I bet she'll be calm soon." Fan said, "Let's wait an hour and try visiting again."

So began what stretched into a six-week vigil, during which Fan only returned to her own home twice, for a total of eight days, once when her mother was discharged to an Alzheimer's facility and things seemed stable, and again just before her mother died. After five days in the Alzheimer's place Patty vomited what a nurse called "coffee grounds emesis," and she sent Fan's mother by ambulance back to St. Jude's. Jack too came for most of this time. Fan's mother was finally sent to a hospice center, where she died after four days. The prognosis was that she had a month or two to live, so when she died Fan had just returned home again.

Only on a few occasions did Fan's mother truly calm down. The hospital staff gave her so much Haldol to get her through her MRIs and other tests (the nurses called it giving her "an overdose of Haldol") that on those days Fan's mother dulled to a syrupy semi-lucidity.

Fan sat with her mother after an MRI one day, and Patty told her dreamily, "If you can't be good be careful," adding, "my mother used to say that." Patty lifted a hand in the gesture of one swearing an oath. "True story!" She had taken to doing this, seeming to feel doubt breathing from her auditors. "They really make those German Mercedes-Benzes in Tuscaloosa," she said a few minutes later, adding, "True story!"

Patty gestured to the hallway and asked if Fan could see the forest fire raging there. Fan said in fact she could not. It didn't seem to bother her mother particularly, as she then fell asleep.

Awake and not too drugged, Patty accused Fan's father of having found someone else, wanting her dead. She accused all of them, even

Jack, of wanting her dead. Though she also asked Jack if he would marry her.

"I'm going to die if you leave me here," she said again and again, her eye fixed on her husband's face. "And you don't look too unhappy about it either. You don't look too broken up."

She screamed, moaned, and threw punches at the nurses and aides and now and then at her family. Or she would beg them to take her home. Fan and Jack came to call her states EM for Exorcist Mom and PM for Pitiful Mom. She switched between the two and they texted each other with updates. *Warning, Flass, we're EM this afternoon.* Fan and Jack fell back into their shorthands, if grim ones now.

Fan recalled combing her mother's hair on her last visit home, her mother's relish of her hands, the Shakespeare quote, the spiritual her mother trilled as she slumped along with her walker: a song that seemed to foretell her death and her acceptance of it. She sang it as she moved, pushing with all her humped energy into the next world. Then Fan sensed something closer to contentment in her mother than she'd ever sensed before.

She remembered telling Paul on the phone that her mother was the poster child for memory being overrated. Now her mother lived the clone type of life again: misshapen, senseless, all swell and grotesquerie.

When heavily tranquilized, her mother Patty mumbled to herself, her hands shook badly, and she slept. Now and again Patty said things that sounded normal. Whatever, they tended to reflect a profound— much more than before the hospital—loss of memory, but other than that, mostly curiosity.

"What does Paul do?" she asked Fan. She recalled Fan's husband existed, but not much more.

"He's a professor," said Fan.

"Wow!" said Patty. "Tell him congratulations for me!" though of course her mother had never known Paul as anything else. Then she said, "Do you think Paul would come and get me out?"

She asked Patrick one morning, "How old are you?" and added, "And when did your hair turn white?"

"Since you got in here," muttered Patty-the-Second, as she couldn't hear him anyway.

Fan's mother seemed like a marionette, Fan thought (and Jack agreed), with some puppet master pulling the flailing raging strings, then the bent and pleading strings, the random question strings. And these last could feel less random than like Fan's mother trying to answer thoughts that might have weighed on her, secretly, her whole life. They had a whiff of the existential about them: what did other people do? Why did they get old? How would you paraphrase peoples' lives?

But the answers: these never quite seemed what she wanted.

"What about Frances?" Patty said suddenly to Glo one afternoon, as Glo came to sit with her (and since Patty had forgotten who Glo was, to whom did she think she directed this question?). Fan had left her father sleeping in the caretaker's center, and she stood outside her mother's doorway, listening.

"You know," Fan heard her mother say, "she doesn't seem anything like me at all."

Through all this Fan and her father and Jack begged for but never got anything that resembled a diagnosis. The urinary tract infection cleared. The MRIs showed Patty had not had a stroke. Fan and Jack could never get the doctors to read her charts.

"What about the blindness?" Fan asked over and over, and more often than not the daily doctor would answer, "But wasn't she blind already in that eye?"

Fan studied her mother's chart, looking up medical abbreviations on her phone, marking pages with relevant information to show the next one. If a nurse or doctor left notes down near her, she grabbed them and copied them.

"It says bell," she told a doctor one day. "Is that Bell's palsy?"

"No," the doctor said, today an ash-haired woman. "It means belligerent."

And so Fan's mother's vision of herself as trapped by accident in the hospital came to have its truth, though a truth created by her rage at her belief she'd been trapped in a hospital. Her hospitalization had been to give her a day or two of IV antibiotics for the urinary tract infection, but within forty-hours of her arrival it became clear she'd never return home. Even on her normal dose of tranquilizer, she lashed out verbally as well as physically. With a Puerto Rican nurse, Fan's mother mocked and exaggerated her every word at an eerie high pitch.

Fan: What Comfort to This Great Decay May Come

"Get that stringy hair out of my face!" she yelled at a nurse who wore long thin braids. "They need to make you cut that dirty stringy hair."

"Mom, her braids are beautiful, don't say that," Fan said, but the nurse, a young and pretty woman with a West African accent, only shrugged.

One day Fan and Jack found their mother with a plum-sized bruise on her blind eye, a black eye that Fan noted to herself was the first one she'd ever seen that was literally black. The staff all claimed not to have seen what happened.

"Maybe she slammed her face down on her food tray," said an aide, and Fan and Jack looked at each other: maybe one of the workers couldn't take her mother's insults anymore. And in fact, when the Alzheimer's facility returned her mother to the hospital for vomiting, it wasn't clear that they needed to. The staff seemed overwhelmed by her, her fury only exaggerated by her tiny size.

When no one was around, Fan's mother turned her hands on herself: her face lay open with long self-inflicted scratches.

And they sat with her. Day in and day out. Fan played *Crawling*. She read articles in magazines that she bought at the hospital shop, mostly about celebrities, Leo who wouldn't settle down, Daniel who did, the Crawleys, who settled and resettled.

She showed her mother photographs, said whatever, just to keep pictures and sound in the air.

"'What comfort to this great decay may come,'" she said to her mother one day, "'must be applied.' That's from *Lear*." Fan's mother tilted her eye her way, a hazel eye, flecked and wet as a pebble on the beach. Occasionally she could hear, sometimes if you shouted, and sometimes for no reason at all.

"Lear," said Fan's mother. "Those daughters."

"Take me home," Fan's mother begged all the time in that stretched falsetto. "Why won't you take me home?" To Fan she yelled, "You're my daughter and you have to do what I tell you."

You're worthless, she screamed at Fan's father and Jack and Fan, *you're useless*.

It felt breathtaking, in a way, for Fan: terrible, but with a kind of terribleness she associated with myth, with stories of encountering Zeus in his godly form, or grasping the monster in your arms as it lashed its many arms or heads but gave you the weapon or the words you needed. Meaningful in some way, like the random meaning spilling from her mother on her last visit. And the anger. The woman her mother had been beneath that still, held surface twisted out from under the surface and into life. Her jealousy, her angst at being ignored, distrust of people different from herself: things you could sense her whole life long, now palpable.

"When did your mother become the Oracle of Delphi," Paul said one day on the phone, on hearing Fan's mother's mystically odd comments. Fan found this astute.

Fan's father tried to deal with his wife's rages by leaving the room, telling her, *If you talk to us this way you gotta stay alone.* He told Patty she was being *persnickety*.

Of course, Fan's mother then wept and begged them to come back. And after that she forgot the lesson of the leaving and it all started again.

If Fan's mother allowed it, Fan held her hand. Generally her mother wanted this and held her hand out as Fan approached. One day, alone with her mother, as her mother raged and wept at once, Fan took her mother's shoulders and pressed her mother's upper body to herself. She curved her hand along her mother's neck, holding Patty's head to her shoulder. Her mother swung and caught a ragged nail along Fan's upper arm, though she didn't seem to do this on purpose. It stung and Fan felt the seep of blood but held. Suddenly her mother's body stopped its juddering and its moan. Patty stilled like a stunned animal, limp, tucked into her body. She moved her head gently, drying her eyes on Fan's blouse. She closed them and her breath slowed. Fan looked down on her, this strange, frizzled head she held, not quite loved, and in her charge wholly.

Fan had a vision, a queasy one, of herself with her mother when she was a little baby. This was what her mother had to do, hold and calm her, feeling as distant from her, as unimplicated by her existence, as Fan felt now about her. Still having to pick the burden up. And for so much longer than any burden Fan might lift. Her mother had not asked for the infant she got, for the feelings she got, whether it be Jack or her, love or its absence. Her response, Fan saw, was the opposite of selfish, was like nothing Fan had ever thought.

Fan: What Comfort to This Great Decay May Come

Patty had no ability to grasp that one eye had gone blind. She must, Fan thought, have imagined part of the world had been erased: a long smear down half of it, like a half-cleaned chalkboard. The one eye unmoored and rolling, the other fixed, fierce. They'd become like a planet and its revolving moon.

Patty's blind eye watered and if she touched her cheek she'd say to her family, *You see, you are making me cry.* Though they weren't tears, not emotional ones anyway, trickling nonstop from her bad eye. Her brain had become so divorced from her body and what it meant.

One day Fan's mother held her good eye on Fan and said (though Fan had not been laughing, or even smiling), "Don't you laugh at me, Frances, you have my genes. You're going to end up just like me."

Patty's blind eye fixed on a spot near the ceiling, while the seeing one held her. Or, Fan thought, the blind eye rolled, looking into the future: her words had the air of prophecy. Oracle of Delphi indeed. Fan felt suddenly peeled of her outer self, raw before her mother.

Then Patty lost her train of thought and said, "I like your shoes. I can't get around in heels anymore, not very well." Though Patty hadn't walked on her own in years. And Fan became herself again.

What killed Fan's mother, ultimately, wasn't cancer or the urinary tract or anything related to her initial hospitalization. Patty began bleeding internally, hence the coffee grounds vomit—the tarry stuff held thick blood. Within ten days, she died. On the night she died, Jack and Fan's father had been sitting with her, but they'd left around ten o'clock. Suddenly Patty's breath clutched, shook itself in her throat.

"Help me, help me," Patty said, and the nurse with the braids—the only person present—cradled Patty in her arms as Patty died. The nurse's hair must have fallen once again across Patty's face, but she only said "thank you": her last words.

The nurse wrote this down—*help me help me thank you*—on a sheet torn from a yellow legal pad, and left them on Patty's side table, with the heading *Last Words* and her name signed, in a quick scrawl, at the bottom. Lisa or Liza something, RN. Fan imagined the staff being trained to take down last words, preserve them instantly no matter how boring.

Doctors could not pin down where the blood inside Patty came from, but something inside her had ripped and her liquids flooded their banks. It was quite possible—"probable, even," Fan said to Paul—that Patty ruptured due to the agitation and the thrashing and the whole reaction created by the hospital stay. If she'd had IV drugs at home, she might well be fine.

"Loopy," Fan added, "but fine." The lesson is, she told him, no hospitals. "Seriously Paul," she said, "it's worth getting a gun to have around for a time like this."

He hung up, then called her back and told her he was coming home. His work in the lab was done, he said. He could review the research they were submitting at home.

Fan's mother wished to be cremated, but before the cremation Fan's father arranged what he called a *viewing* of her mother's body at the funeral home. Paul had not arrived yet. Fan had driven back to her home after checking her mother into hospice care, thinking her mother had more time. Instead she got the news from Jack of her mother's death and rushed back, speeding to get to the funeral parlor, which promised to stay open until she arrived. After that night, there would be no viewing, and no one needed to tell her why, with an untreated corpse. Her mother died in the late afternoon and Fan arrived by eight. Jack met her at the door of the funeral home.

"Where is he?" she said.

"Who?"

"The now-Patty-the-Only."

Even Paul would have found that joke offensive. Jack laughed. "He went home."

A woman opened the funeral parlor door for them, a dark-haired woman in a navy suit. "Come on, Mom is this way," she said, and Fan wanted to yell, *how do you know I called her Mom, and even if I did, she's not Mom now, she's a thing,* but that was irrational, so she simply followed. Her mother lay on a table in an inner room with a blanket up to her chest. The room had been furnished like a living room, with striped sofas at the front. Fan touched her dead mother's face. She took her fingers and brushed her mother down the cheekbone. Of course she knew the dead would be cold. She had felt this cooling with several of her animals, a calico cat for instance, who she had had to have put down due to cancer. Fan corrected herself; she'd had the cat killed. It was necessary, but it was death.

Her mother though had an aggressive coldness. Like marble or coins, dead people seemed to be colder than the things around them, notably cool on the fingertips compared to whatever else you touched. Fan looked at her mother's hands, folded together, and stroked them. It was hard to imagine they'd been moving just days ago, lashing out, or swearing to the truth of her words, stirring the air.

Looking at the crossed wrists and their stillness Fan felt how much effort it had taken for them to move—what a demanding fire had had to burn in her mother's body to keep her warm and moving. Life itself seemed an impossible contraption. Nevertheless, it still worked inside her, unlike her mother.

Her mother had been neatened for the viewing. Her mouth, open at death (according to Jack), had been pressed shut, then stretched out and up at the corners. If you saw this look on a living person, you'd call it a look of contentment (no doubt the idea) but it was not an expression Fan had ever seen on her mother's face. Her mother could smile, and laugh, and had a shrugging twist she gave her mouth at times, but this look of prim satisfaction had never crossed her, any more than had the inner machinations it would take to put it there. Her mother's gray and white hair, wild when she died, had been made neat, but also in a way that did not reflect how her mother looked. They'd pushed it back sleekly from the forehead, though her mother permed her hair and wore it in tight curls around her face. Her mother had a pair of glasses perched on her nose, a pair with heavy frames. The glasses seemed to swallow up her mother's features.

Fan felt that though their intentions were good, the funeral staff had advanced a theory of her mother, of which there was no proof.

Nevertheless, throughout the period of dealing with her mother's death, it had been the body of her mother that obsessed her. Through the planning of the memorial service, the giveaway of her mother's things. Fan in her mind kept seeing her mother on that table and felt a desperate need to go and see her again, long after her mother had been cremated. Sometimes in her head she walked back into that room at the funeral parlor and rearranged her mother's hair, pulled her mouth back to the slightly brooding straight line that would have been natural to her. Other times she sat and talked to her mother's corpse (and how it hurt, still, to use this word in relation to her mother). *How are things there?* she said, and, *now what do you think about everything?* and *Things all turned out ok you know, they really did,* which was a comment on herself and her mother's mothering, but she assumed a dead person would get the nuances. For a response she got that strange contented smile.

Fan's mother's death had taken one day of the year—August 28—and turned it into a death date, a day from then on in shadow. It occurred to Fan that as time passed more and more dates would fall under the same shadow, until finally there would be too many to sustain, and she'd be ready to die herself. That must be how it worked.

And then you'd only be part of other people's time: *this or that happened around the time that poor Frances—*

Your life as someone else's calendar.

Cate: Something Powerful Beyond Measure

Cate lay, chair slats pressing into her back, on the beach in Molokai. The sky shone a hard and expensive blue. A waiter she'd tipped a hundred dollars had set up an umbrella for her and brought her diet Coke after diet Coke. She wore large sunglasses and a long, loose caftan. No one noticed her. Several hotels stood behind her but the landscape was dramatic and not overbuilt, nothing like Waikiki, where she and J once shot a special. This island had white ribbons of beach at the edge of ruffling water, mountains crouched, ribbed and brushy, like green haunches, behind her. Theoretically she was scouting a location for a *Candy and Carlotta* spinoff. She needed to explore a place, get a sense of it, before she could say how it would or would not draw viewers. This one had drama and beautiful colors, but was perhaps a little quiet.

Her assistant Holly, blond, bland, good-natured, actually a high school friend she paid to work for her, made calls for her in her room. Another thing kept muddled on the show: most of the Raws' so-called best friends were actually paid assistants, and most of their assistants had once been friends. Nothing in their world was easy to define.

Cate wanted to be alone for a few days. She had no camera crew. They would never film her checking out a location, making it clear that all their family choices were calculated and show-driven, designed to play in certain ways on viewer emotions.

Cassie had asked to come with her to Hawaii. Cate said no, but Cassie jumped in the car for the ride to the airport anyway *You are getting too hooked on this,* Cassie said, closing the glass between the two of them and their driver.

"On what?" But Cate understood. It reminded her that her mother, jealous and overwhelming as she was, had instincts even her sisters lacked.

"This. You alone. Ducking the crew."

"It's temporary, Mom." On the show she called her mother by the British *Mummie*. "It's just right now I have to think."

So the trip also formed an excuse. Since the night she considered forcing J into rehab, she worried that she needed to do something, to move forward both the show and her marriage. Things were precarious: J could do something utterly unforgivable when drunk, hurt someone, make the news in a way she couldn't control. She needed to rein him in. And she knew her fans expected her to have a child; her sisters had, and they weren't even married. This year she turned thirty-two. But her sisters' having children had made her less, not more, comfortable with the idea. At best, you hatch an unpredictable little being who would look like you before you'd achieved the self you wanted.

She loved her two nieces and her nephew. But if they belonged to her, she had no idea how she'd give them the life she wanted them to have: the one girl resembled her father, with blunt features. The other girl was not model-tall. To be a woman making less of a sensation in the world than her mother had would be intolerable. Her own life often felt redeemed by the volume of ink she got compared to Cassie and her sisters.

A young woman spread a towel down and settled near her on the beach, a woman with a Mohawk and a dragon tattoo. The woman put a cap over her face and lay on her back. Cate had seen dragon tattoos mentioned on a book cover but had never actually seen one. This woman's tattoo seemed huge in relation to her slimness: twining around the curve of her waist from her left side to her right, tail on the left, and on the right the dragon's head reared back, fanged mouth open, as if to swallow her breast.

Cate noticed that each person surrounding her had at least one tattoo, large and complicated. One man had a shoulder tattooed with Celtic knots, the other shoulder bare. Another slightly older man with receding hair had one shoulder covered with a sun surrounded by stylized flames. There was a unilaterality to tattoos, Cate noticed—they climbed up a single calf, or down one arm or shoulder, spread out over one side of a torso. As if the different sides of people asserted themselves.

A man who lay on the opposite side of her, away from the dragon tattoo lady, rolled over on his blanket, and she saw four lines of text slanted across the left side of his abdomen, in heavy script like calligraphy. "Our deepest fear" it began, ending with "powerful beyond measure." She could not read the rest. The man was young, early twenties, probably, and he wore reflective sunglasses under rolled- up light brown hair. As he positioned and repositioned his body on the towel she kept trying to read the lines of print that made up his tattoo, but she couldn't.

Finally she typed the part of the quote she could see into her phone. She expected to find it was an old quotation, from someone like Shakespeare. Or the Bible. Instead it turned out to be contemporary, from a woman named Marianne Williamson, a name she recognized but could not quite place. *Our deepest fear is not that we are inadequate,* the whole thing read. *Our deepest fear is that we are powerful beyond measure. It is our light, not our darkness that most frightens us.* The source was a book titled *A Return to Love.*

Cate remembered that the woman had written books, but also declared she wanted to run for president. When told she'd never make it, the woman said, Well, I'll do something else political. This is my path.

Cate looked over at the young man and confirmed that indeed these very words lined one side of his chest. As she saw this he turned over again, leaving her only his bare side. His chest showed, and Cate saw the same sparse spit-curls that J had.

He must be afraid to forget this fear and power idea, she thought, though he could not read it easily on himself, as the writing stood; the words disappeared around his torso. He'd need a mirror. Did he have to take his shirt off to remember his power, she wondered, or only touch the writing? Or maybe the memory of the tattooing itself—the needle-drill the tattooist used to pierce skin, the way the words would have wept blood for a little while—had made it so he could not forget.

The quote went on, after the end of the part that wrapped across the man, to say *We ask ourselves, Who am I to be brilliant, gorgeous, talented, fabulous?* Cate could understand why the man had chosen not to have this part tattooed on his body, or (if he had) put in some discreet place. Even for an admired person like her, it would be too much.

Cate tried to apply this quotation to herself—what power did she have that might come disguised as a fear? She had the ability to influence people, but only by reading them right and giving them what they wanted. She knew herself this way.

Cate thought, as she watched people pass on the beach, that she understood what it meant to get a tattoo: you were trying to put what was inside of you on the outside. The inner dragon, the knotted spirituality. The words that made sense of something you otherwise might forget.

It became a thought that stuck, with her studying tattoos for where she'd put them on herself, appraising a flight of stars or birds, an orchid or a dove for the way they'd look on her arm, her breast, her leg. She could get filmed getting the tattoo, or just show it off one day, or even keep it secret—something small that could be covered with makeup in a photo shoot.

Then one morning at breakfast she remembered an article she'd read about the most tattooed man in the world, a man featured in Ripley's.

Dennis Avner, known as Stalking Cat, felt like a tiger and had had every inch of himself tattooed with stripes and markings, and had even had holes inserted in his cheeks to screw in whiskers. He had all this done over years—without anesthesia, since no plastic surgeon would do this. Only tattooists. He lived his dream. And then he killed himself by shooting himself in the face. All that was inside of him was outside, and then he destroyed it.

Cate turned off the alerts she had on her phone, for herself and her family. She'd been feeling time closing around her, squeezing: the three days to scout location, the twenty minutes per episode versus the hundreds of hours of film, the few years when she could still expect to be fertile, the handful of hours till J got drunk again.

She stopped in a bookstore and picked up a novel, and a book on time called *Time Travel in Einstein's Universe* by astrophysicist Richard Gott. She riffled through it on the beach. The book argued for the possibility of time travel, because, Gott argued, time itself has no reality anyway, away from the illusion of its presence on the earth. The past, the present, the future, flow and swirl together, like curving streams of water. He quoted a man named Julian Barbour and later Cate found an interview with Barbour on You Tube. Maybe after all the squeeze of time had no merit. Barbour called time not sequential but existing all at once on a cosmic scale, our moments like postcards laid out on a table.

On Cate's last morning in Molokai, a Middle Eastern family appeared and took the spot next to her on the beach, spreading out with an umbrella and chairs. There were two daughters, around eight or nine years old. All three of the women wore the burkini, an outfit that looked like a heavy wetsuit made of cloth, as well as a head covering. Cate noticed how everyone avoided this family; no one sat within ten feet of them except her. Women pointed to the wife and the daughters and whispered, pulling faces at one another. Though the girls played and laughed and pushed each other into waves and seemed happy, and their father smiled at them with appreciation, and listened with interest to his wife when she spoke.

The younger daughter acted like she envied the older's head covering, which had a red stripe down the sides. She tugged at it, took it off her sister and tried it on. She ran her finger down the red stripe.

A Japanese family, a couple with a toddler that could have been any gender, sat behind Cate. It occurred to her that around the time of World War II everyone on the beach would have treated the Japanese family the way they now treated the Middle Easterners, and they would have been just as certain they had good reason. In sixty more years, their reactions to the Middle Eastern family would be as strange and hard to imagine as a judging of the Japanese, who laughed over a newspaper together, and took pictures.

Did this prove Gott's and Barbour's timelessness? No, it reinforced time, how it came and was not fluid but rather, unrelenting. In the future people would watch archives of her show and wonder how she could possibly have thought as she thought and how she could have lived the way she did, or why people cared about her as they did, because people always looked at the past this way—as a kind of kindergarten period of humanity, all magical thinking and optimistic blundering.

That quaint Cate would be the lasting Cate, not the Cate who was modern.

And folks in the future would be right about her but wrong about themselves. They too would see themselves as the people in eternally modern dress.

She called Holly. They'd made plans to drive, before leaving, to an empty cliff-bound beach, where she could stand alone and practice her screaming. Honestly, she doubted she'd take the role she'd been offered in a B movie, *Blood Gifts*. To see her die she sensed would upset something real but subtle with her fans. She might show up for a few days of filming, become exhausted, and perhaps, check into a hospital. Create some drama out of it, and finally, bow out. But she loved rehearsing for her gory death: her normal tone of voice stayed almost a monotone.

And so: a scream flew from her throat like a lit bird. She stood where the waves slapped down and used them as her cue. When the green glassy curve of water rose before breaking, she opened, screamed through the lace creep of the surf, stopped with the sudsy withdrawal. She thought of the tattoo, of the light inside herself that frightened her, and it merged into the white sun broiling into her head and powered her yell. The petrels and albatrosses skimming toward the crouching cliffs flapped off. Holly, ponytail swinging in the wind, looked bored, attempted to grin as Cate watched her, then looked worried as Cate held her eyes but would not smile or speak.

Cate continued to scream, even through the three o'clock rain, punctual and falling onto her like running silver threads. Little bubbles appearing, then things breathing through the sand. As her scream heaved over and over—huge and rude—she thought of time again. Maybe it could be like this, seeming to hang in the air even as she finished. The sound as she got used to it both real in her ears, and not.

Holly ran over. (Are you alright, Cate? Isn't this enough? Lord, you're going to lose your voice *totally*.) Holly needed work done on her chin, Cate thought, ignoring Holly and yelling again. And without Cate, Holly would be no one. Cate did not usually think this way. But she did now. She was like those people in the future, looking down on Holly as from a great distance, noticing her flawed particular face.

Shay, she said to Holly, lisping a bit, time to go, really? Sho shoon?

PART IV

A Butterfly's Wings

The lab's pluripotent cells became stem cells, and then other cells, like heart cells, bubbling out into new forms in their dishes, or so Fan imagined. Paul returned from Scotland. His name was, as he'd wanted it to be back in Korea, all over the newspapers, along with those of his fellow cloners. The stories called this the start of a new age in medicine, though Paul told Fan that they were far from knowing how to make these cells work in the body. And though the news coverage of him wasn't incorrect, he returned with no taste for notoriety, and avoided talking to reporters. Though as the lead American in the group, he sometimes had to. He got relentless polite nagging from the lab's publicist, a Scottish woman named Meg, who talked about "rebranding after Dolly" and sounded very American, though she wasn't.

"And what has it come to when labs hire publicists," he complained to Fan.

Paul came back wanting to focus on Fan, on her mother's dying and what he perceived as her depression after, though Fan did not agree she was depressed. His efforts at support mostly annoyed her. She had no desire to relive the experience of the death by talking about it. And she wouldn't allow the kind of sentimental glossing that he and others fell into, telling her how her mother really loved her, or how her mother must have been proud of her, and so on. Fan became like a merciless teacher, cutting down his comments.

"There's no evidence of *that*," she told him, "so let's not even, okay?"

Fan considered what she would do to end her life if she thought she was getting Alzheimer's. She tried to hide these meditations, but they broke out: "How many rocks in your pockets would it take exactly, to sink into the River Ouse?" she'd ask, thinking of Virginia Woolf's suicide.

It was this line of thinking that Paul identified as depression, though it wasn't, just trying to find a tolerable way she could live the rest of her life in her body, with its mother-haunted, mother-cursed genes.

Paul became fascinated by shrubs, drinks based on fruit syrups and vinegar. He made them from scratch, chopping fruit into a saucepan with boiling water and sugar. Fan had not seen him moving around a kitchen in many months. She'd forgotten how tenderly he could dispatch that which was also tender. He held a pear in one hand cupped like a new kitten, cut pieces perfectly even, though he cut only to drop them into boiling water. His hands trained by handling pipettes and needletips and pinpoint ova and nuclei, decades of tiny delicate things.

His finished drinks—like a pear shrub with raspberry vodka—always smelled sweet in the making but tasted sour.

They talked, more honestly than they had before, though a sense of artificiality hung over their routine: they ate when they had before, had drinks likewise. She made the fresh tomato sauce with olives and basil that she always made in late summer. On a warm evening, if they would in the past have sat in the garden on their bench, they would sit in the garden on their bench. Fan was teaching a course on Shakespeare's tragedies and Paul asked her how it was going, how the students liked the film she showed them of *Macbeth*. He asked how she helped her students understand the plays as theater—lines of script—when they read them on the page. It felt like a loaded question, though not deliberately so: the lives they fell back into felt scripted. That Fan had co-written the script did not make it any less alien.

"Should we sit outside?" said Paul one evening, and she noticed how they'd fallen into the language of should and shouldn't: they hadn't asked each other what they wanted for a long time.

"Would you like to?" she said. He looked at her.

After a simple disposition of her mother's ashes into a gray, logy river near her parents' house, Fan went home. Paul had come for the service but did not return with her for the disposition.

"We threw it off the bridge by the house," she told Paul briefly of the ash. He'd been busy with a burst of media interest in the cloning story and had agreed to appear on two morning television shows. Paul had become more reconciled to his role as cloner-on-call for the media. He still felt guilty and imposter-y, he told Fan, but Fan could see part of him turning on to his Warhol's share of fame. Paul had become so engrossed with it that he forgot to ask about Fan's mother and the ash disposal, which Fan felt grateful for. Paul's parents were living. And he was not a person who would get the psychological pull of a can of burnt matter.

"It's absurd, they ask the most ridiculous questions," he told Fan of his interviews. "Like, 'If I'm dying can I just clone myself?' 'I think I have the most wonderful son in the world, can I just make him a twin?' It's not like they even think that, they just want to give their viewers some big quotable thing. I have a little memorized speech about gene expression. So I'm giving it this morning to Wendy Rose and she says, all naive-like, 'Well, how can you call it cloning if you don't end up with a clone?'"

"Jeez."

"I said, 'Of course it's a clone. A clone just isn't what you think it is.' I tried to show her the CC cat photos but she was off onto something else, this 'When do you think cloning will be a part of all of our lives' question."

"Just tell them what they want to hear," said Fan. "'I'm having myself cloned. My clone's growing even as we speak.'" She paused and began twining her hair into corkscrews with a finger, imagining life with curly hair. "Tell them, 'Next time around my clone's doing the interview with you.'"

"'He'll be genetically enhanced to answer stupid questions.'"

"Right."

"I met someone in the Green Room of the *AM Chatter*," Paul said. Fan could hear a rise in the pitch of his voice, a sign that this for him was the high point, the precious tidbit, of the conversation. "Someone you find really interesting. Cate Crawley."

"No way, you're kidding." Cate had come into Fan's mind that day on the bridge. She seemed like someone who wouldn't be reducible to such a canister of leavings, if only because parts of her body were plastic. And there would be someone in her life—some adviser or assistant—who would have known the right thing to do with a mother's cremains.

"No, I'm not kidding, and she was sweet, in a friendly cat sort of way, holding a lot back maybe, but interested. And smarter than you'd think," said Paul. "She asked a lot of intelligent questions."

"Like what?"

"Oh, I don't remember." Fan could tell at once that he did but wanted to sound like it hadn't mattered to him all that much.

"What did she look like?"

"She was beautiful, but looking at her I felt like I was seeing her through a screen. She's so flawless she looked flat."

Fan remembered the time when, watching Cate on television, Cate had come alive for her. The sense of them as human together, moist, muggy, light hitting the eye, which batted it backward to the brain, making pictures. Sorting through them, half-aware. The contraption-like grinding on of the body, whether one put on lipstick or just blinked an eye.

So much had happened since that moment. Settling in Korea, sex with Peter, and her husband's lie. Funny that she had never looked at her husband Paul with the same understanding of their shared humanness.

She imagined Cate and Paul in a room together, Paul looking down uncomfortably, feeling Cate existed in a different world. And Fan wondered if Cate still understood herself as human, or if, as celebrities must, she felt she'd transcended into some other form of existence. Her image reproduced exponentially around the world, so many Cates living in superposition with one another. Fan had a sudden fierce desire to meet the woman.

Cate had said to him, "This matter of children is entirely too random," thinking as she said it that it didn't sound like her. The man, the clone scientist named Paul—scheduled to appear briefly on the show before her—obviously had little experience with television. He worked his face like someone who didn't think much about having a face, and who had no clear vision of that face from the outside. He held his mouth with the teeth too close together, an expression that further puffed out already puffy cheeks. He kept his eyes downward—shyly, thought Cate—and should have widened them and looked straight ahead; the eyes were a nice hazel color, but small. His brows reminded her of her Tita's, heavy and natural. She wished she could share his obliviousness to how often he blinked.

When a camera turned on, she automatically counted blinks, doling them out as her eyes grew irritated. Off the air she remained aware of them, slowing her blinking when she first turned her eyes toward someone.

A Butterfly's Wings

The green room had sofas, and on a table, coffee mugs with *AM Chatter* stamped on them with quick-scribble caricatures of the two hosts, a man and a woman. And there was a bowl with miniature candies. The man, Paul, took a mug and put it carefully into the backpack he had with him—they were souvenirs and it wasn't theft, though Cate would never dream of taking something like that, of seeming to want it. He unwrapped a mini Kit-Kat.

"I can figure out how to make my life work. I can't figure out how to make someone else's," said Cate. "That's what I mean about children."

And he said around his Kit-Kat, "Ah. I've never wanted children," which she took to mean: I get your point.

"What they say is if your kid's not happy, you can't ever be happy. Never again." Cate looked at Paul, half-expecting him to confirm or deny this. "That's what my mother and my sisters say.

"And if you do what works for you, and it doesn't work for them, how can you forgive yourself," Cate went on. She'd been trying to engage Paul in the eye contact with which she launched any interaction—a direct slightly widened wash of gaze—but his eyes stayed low and avoided hers.

Cate had been thinking a lot about children lately. She both wanted them and wanted what they could do for the show and her marriage and did not want the soup of features and qualities her sisters had birthed. It felt like there should be another way. Paul had explained that he was on the show to talk about cloning, and that human cloning was all they wanted him to talk about, though he worked with medical cloning and animal cloning only.

Cate said, "I can see why cloning yourself attracts people. It's not that you wouldn't love any child, but you'd love them and have no idea how to help them, if they felt really different from you."

"The truth is," the man said with a slight air of the rote, "there's this thing called gene expression."

"Oh, I know. Not all the genes are turned on."

"Sure." He looked up at her and she could see she'd surprised him. "Your child would get all of your genes but that's way more genes than she'll ever use. It's kind of like ideas. You have hundreds of them but just act on two or three. Your clone would never be just you."

Cate heard the wild ambiguity of these words in this context: Not be her in the sense that she existed now, with all her plastic surgery?

Not be her because this child would grow up in a different environment than Cate had? Or not be her because for this child the camera would be present from birth on?

"I wouldn't want my child to *be* me, exactly," said Cate. "Just close. It seems weird that with all we know we can't just turn on the genes we want."

"No, the science for that is . . . far away. Any clone of yours would be more likely to be like you than a regular child. Or more like your mother or your sisters. Those would be some of the genes potentially on offer."

"They could get good genes from me, I guess. I mean find good things I didn't know were there."

"There's that." Paul pulled out of his backpack a photograph of a cat, a gray tabby.

"She's a clone. Her name is Copy Cat." He put the photo on the table in front of Cate. "Her clone mother's a calico."

Cate realized she had raised her brows a titch, so she leaned back and tucked each brow down in turn, a gesture she'd done a hundred times for the camera.

Paul slowly unpeeled another Kit-Kat. *Such a civilian*, Cate thought. That was the term she used in her head, not just for an ordinary person, but for a person who wouldn't know how to take a selfie, do Instagram, or Photoshop. A person who lived directly reactant to the body: felt life inside out, not outside in. If he craved a bite of cheap chocolate, he'd grab a Kit-Kat. Cate noticed when the man stopped to think, he clenched his teeth, doing his cheeks no favors. She imagined he wondered if she wanted more details about cloning and genes.

"My wife really likes you," Paul said suddenly. Then he looked embarrassed. Cate had seen this before—men told her this about their wives, then worried she'd infer they themselves didn't like her.

"I'm glad," she said. "Women are really what I care about. Tell me about your wife."

"I took this coffee mug for her," said the cloner, and he seemed to take a second to notice that he hadn't answered the question. "Her mother just died. Her mother had dementia and she got very angry and accusatory and it was a hard death." It seemed to register, in a twist of the man's mouth, that he still hadn't really described her. "She has a very dry sense of humor. She likes physics and Shakespeare. Time theory lately."

"I've heard Julian Barbour," said Cate. "He thinks each moment exists forever, like Polaroids." She considered this for a second, considered the moments they reshot and reshot. Was she somehow more existent for this? "And me. She likes me?"

"Yes. She'll be jealous that I met you."

"A hard death," said Cate. "I'm sorry. Give me her address. I'd like to send her a note of sympathy." Paul scrawled on a business card and handed it to her.

"I know this town," said Cate. "My art buyer's in Eder. I'll be doing a meet-and-greet there." Paul looked at her uncomprehendingly.

"My wife used to work in Eder," he said. "A hotel maid." He added quickly, "You know, to get through school."

"I was a personal assistant for three years," Cate smiled at him. "I get being in service." It was not at all the same,of course. But she practiced finding in herself these little relational moments, passing them along, like lengths of rope to haul in the people she met.

Fan took a train to the station in Eder, walking to the Mariposa with an overnight bag. In a few hours Paul would meet up with her. She felt silly going to a hotel so near her own town, so she packed a bag that looked like a large purse. But she had little chance of running into anyone she knew. She was long out of touch with her few sort-of friends. Fan passed under elms and sweet gum trees, leaves drying on the branch, not yet all-coloring. Sweet gum spikes hung like earrings, and she crushed the five-pointed leaves in her hands for the odor, resinous as Greek wine.

Yellow yellow red and yellow. Yellow being the remains of color, after the green mask of chlorophyll dropped away. The leaf done with its work, its color like an unmade-up face. She thought of her fall in Seoul, the red maple leaves, the sense of life ramping up, instead of, as now, decelerating into yellow, into the limbs, the bones of things.

The sweet gum fresh in her nose, along with the peaty odor of fallen leaves. Strange to think of the frantic vibration going on in there, just to bring this odor to her, so she could choose to ignore it, or not. And if she chose to recognize it, idly inhaling to pass the scent a little deeper before her senses, then ions in her brain misting through their voltage channels to give to her senses that odor. All the improbable tiny processes that define being alive. Fan had the sense again of her body grinding on, an elaborate contraption. Possibly so we can think about the elaborate-contraptionness of it all.

A bizarre property appeared ... some of that matter became aware. The function of this odd property isn't at all clear. Where had she read that?

Fan thought of Donald Hoffman, his belief that all our reality is a user interface, manifested by us, and radically simplified from whatever might really exist in the world. She crushed another leaf in her hand, a leaf of a bright almost pulsing yellow, with an overwhelming scent. Spicy and pleasant, but if it were a food, you wouldn't eat it; your mouth might taste of it forever. The possible simplification of things felt in this moment like a small blessing.

Though math couldn't be simplified by perception and instead would yield the brain-hurtingly complex nature of things. Even without any knowledge of math, Fan sensed this was true.

Once Paul had sent Fan an invitation to dinner at his house. Like their drinks, the invitation—actually a copy of *Feynman's Lectures on Physics,* sent through inter-university mail, with highlighted words and letters—formed an elaborate code. The words and letters had to be assembled using the order of the colors of the rainbow—red orange yellow green blue indigo violet—to make sense of the highlighted text, otherwise not in any order. It came with the clue *where pots containing gold are found you will find how to read me.* When she'd puzzled it out, which took several days, it said, with a few puns on *magnetism* and *momentum,* simply, *Come at seven for dinner and be hungry. Wear red.*

The complexity of the invitation just there to show how much she was wanted. She began to feel the same towards the intricate workings of her body.

She had not reacted to Paul's invitation with any kind of extravagance. *Red?* she asked and he answered, *tomato sauce.* Okay then, she said. Alright. Yes.

Fan had gotten a note from Cate, the script large, round, and childlike, though she doubted it was Cate's own. Probably an assistant's. *Thank you for being a fan,* it read, and *I feel for you in your grief. My fans are my family.* Somewhere in Cate's home, which was also her business, no doubt were pages of standard notes for her staff to copy. Fan had not imagined this part of Cate's life, but like any public person, like a politician, Cate needed to feed the sense of relationship with the people who put her where she was.

Cate or Cate's surrogate tucked into the card a ticket, stamped *Free Pass* with the date and time of a meet-and-greet of Cate's at the Baums store in Eder, an event occurring in two weeks. The ticket was small and red and looked exactly like an old-fashioned movie ticket. When Fan told Paul about the free pass he said, "Do people actually pay for that kind of thing?," and without waiting googled the answer. It turned out they did. Sometimes they just paid a few hundred dollars, sometimes they bought merchandise. Access to Cate in this case depended on going to a counter with a receipt showing you'd spent at least $500 on Crawley clothes at that store in the past week. You could exchange the receipt for a ticket, limited supply. Of course, Fan with her pass did not have to.

"Are you going?" asked Paul, and before she answered said, "At least you won't have to buy any of those clothes."

"And how would you know about the Crawley line?"

"I've seen things," said Paul, who then took a frank hard bite from the knuckle of his pinkie. "They can hardly be called *clothes*. They're like latex gloves for the body."

It was Fan's idea to stay at the Mariposa. She guessed if Cate Crawley were going to stay in town that's where she'd stay and, in any case, she liked the idea of being in walking distance of Baums.

"It will be fun. We could have like a little honeymoon," she told Paul. Paul ran his hands along the beard he was trying to grow back in, the same fine but glittering red-brown along the jawline he'd had when they first dated. She thought for a second and said, "I'll reserve the tub room." And Fan imagined how she and Paul could use the tub and the room to work an object magic that would undo all she'd done—that still pricked her inside—in the sarang bang in Korea. Though of course Paul wouldn't be aware of this magic. He would be like an infant, going mindless and unknowing to a transformation like a christening.

"I'll make the reservations," Fan said. "I'll text you what room I'm in after I check in. I'll pack a nightie." And she thought for a second and added, "Bring champagne."

Fan set out for the hotel on a warm, mid-September day. The news of Cate's visit managed to reset her inside, at least for now: in her mind her mother's scratched and blackened face had been replaced with Cate Crawley's mask-like one. The change was pleasant. Fan wore the black bra, still smelling of massage oil with a hint of salt, under her blouse. The tub room had not been available, but she had found another room.

Now clouds hung flush with each other and flat-bottomed in the sky, as if they lay on glass. Cumulus: fluff above the flat line. These kinds of clouds, the hazed blue, made Fan feel like she stood inside a snow globe. She had had many of these as a child, thanks to her aunt Glo, who traveled a bit, and who somehow decided Fan wanted to collect snow globes. Fan did not. But Fan could see how her aunt wanted only to buy these things, not keep them. Perhaps she liked the connection with her name. Mostly the aunt, her father's sister, simply wanted the proof to exist, somewhere, that she'd been places. Fan had a New York skyline snow globe, another from Pensacola Beach. The ocean in the Pensacola snow globe looked like thick blue frosting. One globe from Lourdes showed a young girl kneeling before a large woman in blue and white robes. *Bernadette*, said Glo, and gave her a pamphlet about the girl's visions of the Virgin Mary. According to the pamphlet Bernadette had seen a vision of a woman she described as a "small young lady," so throughout her childhood Fan interpreted the girl kneeling as the holy apparition.

When Glo visited she peeked into Fan's room, where the snow globes lined her pink child's dresser. Glo picked up one or two and shook white on whatever—the Empire State Building, or the Pensacola beach, and its stiff water, which held up little peaks to the snow.

"I like these things," she said, fingertips on Fan's shoulder, then she swept her hand along the display. "Where would you go first?" and Fan looked at New York, Lourdes, Pensacola, and the other places, like Disneyland and Lake Tahoe. Glo liked to think she gave Fan a sense of the world and its possibilities. But these were cramped, cold representations, with snowflakes that, proportionally, would have been big as her palm. And it fell too fast: a quick upending, then a stifling blur. Fan chose a different destination each time her aunt asked, just to make her aunt happy.

Her aunt had grown up not mining herself, but in the same context as Fan's father, in the mining town run mostly by the mining company, a world of people who squeezed themselves daily into the earth, many of them dying there. Or dying above ground, but choking to death on the ore they breathed, which blacked the hidden spaces of their lungs. Fan thought her aunt must go places and still imagine herself squeezed in, above the earth this time but caught: now in glass.

Anyway, on sunny days like this one, when the clouds fleeced above but leveled out on the bottom like they bumped against a clear pane, Fan imagined herself trapped in a globe. And she felt eyes on her, eyes curious to imagine how she'd look with thick white piling on her long dark hair, her shoulders. It was the observer-driven universe; someone looked down on her, shook her world into action.

Fan checked in at the front desk, handing over license and credit card while peering—she hoped casually—around the lobby. She headed down the first-floor hall, though her room lay above; she eyed the restaurant. No sign of Cate.

As Fan walked down the hallway, she noticed a woman in the maid's room, door ajar, and without thinking she pushed on in. Her unsettled life sent her back to earlier habits. When the maid looked up, Fan thought she might have seen this woman around town a few times: about Fan's height, hair a bituminous color, quick in her movements, abstracted. A face very oval, a mark like an upside-down heart by the eye, deep lids. The face felt familiar somehow. Not a feeling that they'd met, exactly, but fuzzier, as if she'd daydreamed her, and now here she was.

The maid clutched a glossy magazine with Cate Crawley on the cover, dressed as the Mona Lisa, but with an enormous amount of breast showing. The cover punned on something Cate's husband J-lord had tweeted: that Cate's body was like a piece of Renaissance art, and not to show it would be to hide a masterpiece.

"Want to share?" The woman held out a cigarette, lighted it with a pink Zippo at Fan's nod. Menthol: herbaceous under the burning. Did she think Fan was a maid, not in uniform? Or didn't she care?

"How is your day going," said Fan.

"Oh," the woman said, "Menza, menz," an Italian phrase people used to mean so-so. She took a careful look at Fan's face, quirked her brow. She seemed to feel Fan had wandered in there to tell her or ask her something.

"It's odd," said Fan. "I worked as a maid here for years. When I saw the door open I wandered in without thinking."

"You can't miss this job," the woman said.

"I can a little," said Fan. "Well, some things." What she missed most had to do with smoking, and would feel strange to mention, now, as they passed the cigarette. So familiar: you curled smoke into your lungs, took the cigarette out of your mouth, eyeing it for a second before giving it over to the two fingers of the other.

"Hmmm." The implication of the sound was lost.

They smoked together. It was understood that they could only take a few drags each. Smoking was not allowed in maids' closets. Still, they did it, the woman holding at the ready a can of Lysol.

"You look familiar to me," said Fan finally.

"That's funny. I thought that about you. Not like I went to high school with you or anything." The woman gave Fan an appraising look. "Maybe like I saw your picture in the newspaper and it stuck with me for some reason."

The maid over-pronounced *picture—pick-cher—*trying to suppress the pronunciation of it as *pitcher,* Fan guessed, which the woman had no doubt grown up with, as had Fan, who completely revamped her pronunciations when she got to college. She had to: sometimes other students couldn't understand her, and sometimes they mimicked her, not kindly. Once at a party a friend slugging rum started spitting out, *It's in the drahhhhh* and it took three or four times before Fan could hear that the word the girl mimicked was *drawer,* and further, that the parody was of herself. As soon as she heard herself from the outside Fan couldn't talk that way anymore, though she couldn't pronounce standard English without sometimes being aware of herself either.

Fan began to talk to this woman about having been a maid, letting her diction go back to its natural place as she described a room she'd once cleaned with a box of butt plugs—all colors and sizes—by the bed. There was a way of saying *butt* here: you popped your lips out at the double-T's. Fan knew through linguistics courses that this was called a glottal stop, though for most of her life she'd just done it. She carefully popped her T's now. As the woman answered, she too relaxed her diction.

"Slob kebobs, right?" she said. "Wouldja believe?" Her sentence endings lilted. "We could write a book." And Fan jumped a little, thinking for a second the woman expected her to, actually, write a book. But no; this was just a saying.

"Do you ever catch the ones that dress up like maids?"

"Ohhhh yeah." The woman smiled without showing her teeth. "We get company every month or so."

"I've never been in the paper," said Fan, letting it go as *pay-puh*. "Maybe in a previous life."

The woman said, very seriously, "I hope in that one I did something more interesting than this."

It occurred to Fan that there were things she could say that might help this woman. That she had a job now where she had more prestige, and worked less than she had as a maid, but didn't make much more money.

She could add that this new life too had become routine, in the same way filling a cart and dispensing its contents and spraying and wiping and vacuuming had. That even her husband who had money—and who was decent and loved her—hadn't worked out the way the woman she was when she cleaned, and her cohort, guessed such a man would.

Fan couldn't imagine how to share what she was thinking. It would be arrogant; she didn't know if this woman had any good moments at her job, as she'd had. Or if she had chances to do anything different. She couldn't even say what she meant by *happy*, a word that dissolved as you looked at it.

So, "What is it about sharing a smoke?" she asked rhetorically, then, "What's your name?"

"Filomena. Mostly I go by Ef."

"I'm Fan." She dragged deeply, watching the ember burn back toward her lip. "When I worked here, all us maids were really friendly."

"That so?" Filomena took the cigarette from her, considering it. Suddenly she smashed it out against the back of her shoe, then slipped it in her apron pocket. "Friendly. I guess, yeah."

"I think I really needed friends back then," said Fan.

"And you don't now?"

"Now . . . I'm married. But no, I do. It's just really different, I guess." Fan missed the cigarette, the way releasing smoke veiled a little the work of releasing words. "I just had a good friend and I lost her because of something our husbands did. The older you get, the more that's going on in your life, the more it gets complicated. With friends." Ef sprayed the Lysol can straight up; Fan could feel little beads landing in her hair. "Actually my husband and I are staying here right now. I was thinking maybe we could work things out better in a different place. Neutral." Fan felt her university diction returning.

"Work things out? Because of what he did? With this friend's husband?" Ef looked into Fan's eyes.

"Yeah, but it wasn't, like, personal, it was business related." Fan thought of Filomena's earlier, expectant look. "I lied to him, he lied to me. Now we don't know what to do."

"Trust. You don't trust each other."

"No, that's the weird thing," said Fan, "we do." Which was true. In spite of—or because of—all that happened, she and Paul had grown open in what they talked about. She'd told him how she understood the role her adjunct status played in his love. He did not disagree. And he told her he knew she often checked their bank account. Now Fan looked at Filomena. Impossible to explain all this.

"I don't know how people have trust and love both," she said finally. "Sometimes I think they sort of cancel each other out. Because you trust what you're used to, don't you, but you don't love what you're used to. You love what's new."

"What I don't get lately is how people believe in things," Ef said. "God, politics, what-have-you." She put a hand inside her outfit and took a long scratch where the built-in apron pressed in. Fan could remember that itch in her own core. The maid went on, "There were some TV preachers I liked but they were just doing this fill-in-the-blank-with-the-right-word thing. You pray this word, you get that."

"Wow. Like it's all just a crossword puzzle."

"Yeah. So my parents are Catholics. I was raised in the church. But when you look hard at things you're told, they just don't seem real."

"I was raised Catholic too," said Fan. "My aunts told me if I didn't make a good confession the host would go all bloody in my mouth. I was terrified. But at some point you don't confess something and your mom makes you take communion and you figure out there's no blood, it's really just a cracker."

"I heard that blood thing too," said Ef. "And yeah, I remember bringing a hankie to the altar rail, because I didn't confess to hardly anything. And then I was kind of disappointed."

"Maybe the thing to do is, you don't try to figure it out," said Fan. "You just accept that the world is much weirder than you could ever imagine. Some people think everything possible must be real."

"The Lord our God is a weird god." Ef considered. "Blood from a cracker is weirder than I can imagine."

"It is." Fan looked down at Ef's magazine, ran a forefinger around Cate Crawley's torso, following the plush lines of her breasts and her flat Mona Lisa hair, with a veil laid lightly over it, a veil almost invisible. "I think people like her because she doesn't stand for anything specific. We just notice her."

"Well, she's real. Actually, she's here," said Ef. "She's staying in the tub room. I think. Her people reserved a floor and I understand most rooms will be empty. But that's the nicest one. I'd use it if I were her."

"That's wild," said Fan. "Do you want to see her?"

"Hell yeah. I'm going to sashay past her room wearing one of her dresses. From the store."

"I'm going to see her at Baums. I think."

"There'll be like a thousand people there," said Ef.

Ef had made the offer to share a smoke without thinking. She'd had the strange but distinct feeling that this woman had pushed her way in to the maid's closet to ask her a question. She thought of Tom, of Light and Light's God, for whom the picked-on were special, though not special enough to speak to God in their own words. No one was. God was a being who said things once, perfectly, then hoped to hear his perfect words spoken back to him again and again and again. Like a playwright, like a Shakespeare, who wrote the words and then settled in to hear them at the theater, night after night.

She had thought of the hotel as static, but this woman had come here for something to happen. That much showed in her face.

The woman had gorgeous straight black hair—really black, not dark brown—and her face had a beauty that was the effect of all her features, no one of which stood out. She had full arched brows, dark eyes, a fine straight nose and a wide but not terribly full mouth. All together the woman's face had a striking impact but given how hard to pin down her beauty was, it was possible the woman herself didn't recognize it. Somehow Ef wanted her to recognize it.

The woman traced her finger around Cate on the magazine cover, looking vaguely hypnotized.

"She's beautiful," said Ef. "But so are you."

Ef looked at Cate Crawley. She hadn't realized she was going to dress up and prance by Cate's room until Fan asked.

"That's exactly what my husband would say if he were here." And Fan looked slightly embarrassed.

"You don't believe him?"

"No, I do. I just don't know what it means anymore."

Fan paused, then reached into Ef's pocket for the cigarette stub. "Do you mind? Just a few more puffs? I haven't smoked in ages." She pulled matches from her purse, a pink box, and lit, sucking deep and handing it over. "I hate what's happened with my husband, but the honesty, that's good. I don't know that I could go back. And he's the best person I've ever had a relationship with. By far."

Ef took the cigarette. In high school once she and a bunch of girls had called names at some other girls, shouting *ho* and *dirtbag* and on and on—first as a joke, then it wasn't. A teacher sat them down in an empty room, passing around a piece of chalk that he called the *talking stick*. When you held the talking stick, you had to say what was on your mind and no one could interrupt you. The stubby cigarette felt like a talking stick.

"I date women," Ef said, and while it wasn't true yet it felt true, in a way she imagined words from the Bible could feel true, if you chose right.

Ef expected something to happen. But the woman, Fan, continued to seem absorbed in Cate's breasts, which, to be fair, had a curve along the top that a person would associate not with breasts, but with cantaloupes or with moons. Ef felt lighter.

"Well, that makes the whole Catholic thing harder, doesn't it?" Fan said.

"I guess. Anyway, I've got to get back to work."

Later Ef, slipping Fan's number from the front office and heading to the concierge's desk to text her, wondered what in the world in this circumstance she would write. The woman had seemed almost Mona Lisa-like herself, but with a touch of the mourner about her. Like one of the ladies in the boat.

Fan left the closet and immediately headed to the second floor. Ef's comment about a thousand people worried her. She walked the length of the floor: doors closed, no maids or room service visible; silence. She cupped a hand but could hear nothing behind any of the doors, where she'd imagined nails slicking with polish, toenails buffed, eyebrows filled with a hundred tiny strokes. She knew from the show that women like the Crawleys had many people working on them at once—painting, depilating, curling, spraying, braiding—as if they sat attended by a many-armed goddess or god.

It was two o'clock. The Crawley entourage might or might not have checked in. This was not the sort of event that would appear on the show, one very routine for all the Crawleys, but too pedestrian to air. Who would be here, Fan knew from following the family, would be bodyguards, publicists, hair and makeup people. Assistants.

Then suddenly the elevator doors opened and Fan's fancy strolled out: the magazine cover stretched its hands out from the folded Mona Lisa position; the flat image from television cast a shadow on the floor. Her face was no mask. It had a slight but noticeable aggrieved crumple of the lips.

Though Cate wore only half her face. She had the rimmed eyes with the sleek, multi-toned lids and shaped brows. The rest was unformed, speckled. Cate wore a plain shift like a housecoat, loose and adrift around her famous figure.

"You're Cate Crawley." Fan studied the raw unmade-up part of Cate's face: pores, blotches, features that felt recessed, shy almost, without makeup, except the nose: wider. She shifted her eyes from Cate's eyes and brow to the lower part of Cate's face, taking in the duality: the Cate she knew on top, the Cate she did not know, and wouldn't see again, on the bottom. On the magazine cover Cate had had dark winey lips. Her natural lips almost blended with her skin.

Strangest of all was seeing Cate alone. Never on the show, never in her appearances, did Cate appear as a lone body, but always as one small, overdeveloped female form among a cluster of simpler ones. She stood smaller than Fan by a good inch. Of course, Fan felt how her own body, in proximity to Cate, became something of a foil, the role in the diorama played by the form of the normal human.

Cate watched Fan with her brows raised—a tiny hitch—clearly expecting Fan to state her business: a selfie with her, an autograph.

"Where is everyone?" Fan blurted and realized that the question sounded strange and a little stalker-ish. Cate's pale lips parted, but she stayed silent. She may have believed Fan worked for the hotel.

"I'm Fan. You met my husband Paul on a show. He's a cloner. You sent me a card. I'm going to meet you at Baums but I came here first." Fan felt the dampness on her face before she recognized it as tears, like the stealth tears of the jjimjilbang, or the false tears of her mother. "Cate, my mother died."

She put her head down and wept, as she thought, like an idiot. She found herself in the odd position of telling the Cate in her head the whole story of meeting Cate: *Oh God, then I wept like an idiot.* But Cate was there, waiting mystified, in front of her.

"I felt like you'd be someone I could tell," Fan said finally. "Your grandmother died and all."

"I have had losses," Cate told her. "And my Tita died." Cate coughed lightly. "Is my voice funny? I've been screaming a lot. Not *at* anybody." She smiled and moved toward Fan, passing an arm around Fan's shoulder. To Fan's shock, Cate cradled her, patting her between her shoulder blades. "I do understand, I do, I do."

Fan bent a little, put her hand on Cate's waist, firm but tiny.

Cate's voice poured out with a distinct polish, even around the cough. Fan felt in her cheek the sharpness of the bone at Cate's clavicle, the breast beneath like a firm pillow. She inhaled Cate: some expensive perfume, and beneath that, a personal odor: beach air, musk. Something of those sweetgum leaves, but mammal. Cate indeed was moist and muggy, and into her private light cone proffered a space. It was a shock, that Cate had a physical body.

Cate looked around, as if she expected someone to be there; maybe posing a little. Her lips uncrumpled. Then, "your mother loved you, I'm sure," she said.

"No, she didn't. And she managed to come to terms with that. Which makes it harder."

"Mothers. Well. " Cate slipped a key card from a bag Fan recognized as a Fendi. Cate swiped the door, twisting the knob before glancing over and noticing that Fan still stood there, no doubt looking, Fan thought, absurd and stricken.

"Why don't you come into my room for a minute," Cate said.

Cate led Fan in, with an arm lightly on her shoulder. She walked over to the bed and slid her purse and tote bags down on it from her arm. Fan stayed close to the door, looked around the room: brick-red walls, a bathroom shining out in white and chrome. It had been remodeled since she'd last worked here, elegant, with a black vanity by the tub and a matching dresser. Only the tub was the same, askew toward the window. Where she'd imagined she could bathe the last year of her life out of her pores.

Then Cate took a few steps back toward the vanity, which brought her close to the edge of the tub. She put a hand against its white surface.

"I don't know." Cate grabbed a tube of red lipstick from the vanity and with one hand filled in her lips—the round bottom lip, the upper lip with the sharp arch—expertly, without seeming to notice. The bright mouth brought her close to the Cate of television. "Anyway, I'm sorry about your mother."

"She was in such a rage. There was a nurse with braids, and my mother would yell at her, 'Cut off that dirty stringy hair!' It was awful." Fan stepped forward too, looking into the tub. "Then when my mother started dying she called out 'Help me' and that nurse just wrapped her in her arms. She held her and held her and then my mother died."

Cate looked at Fan as if she herself were working out a problem, like one in math.

"You know," said Cate, "I've been thinking about a man who says there's no such thing as time."

"Julian Barbour?" Cate once again seemed launched from Fan's imagination.

"I've been thinking about terrible things that happen," Cate went on, "like maybe it's different if it's not the end. I mean, what if it wasn't the end, wouldn't that make sense? Maybe that nurse holding her is what she needed, in order to live her life better. Some piece of it."

Cate spread out her arms. "I once did something people think was a bad thing, but then I figured out that it was wrong for when I did it, but for now it's right. And it was about love really." Cate swept a hand through a box on the vanity. "I'm launching a makeup line today. Let me give you something. You can have a nude for your lip, a red for your nails." Cate held out an embossed tube and a red drum-shaped bottle. She flexed her own sheer nails under Fan's eyes playfully. "You can be the opposite of me."

Fan felt her phone vibrate softly against her chest.

Cate swirled a finger around the inside of the tub, as if she were swirling water. "I bet now wherever she is your mother loves you. Or at least she gets you."

This thought was, in its way, both soothing and disturbing. "I wish I had your power to believe that." Fan began edging toward the door. "I should go, I guess."

"It was nice talking to you," Cate said. "My people are going to wait for me out back, at the entrance to the kitchen. Why don't you come with me. We'll go to the store together." Cate gave Fan a practiced wide-eyed look. "In about an hour. I need to get dressed and make a phone call. I doubt I'll be able to talk to you at the store. There'll be like a thousand people."

Fan backed out of the room, without meaning to, but remembering after a second that this was the way people had to exit an audience with British royalty. In the hallway she spun around, reached in her inside pocket for her phone, where she found a message from a strange number: *Yea though I walk through the valley of the shadow of death.*

She dialed Paul. She had forgotten to text him the number of the room. And all this . . . what was all this? She wasn't sure, but she needed Paul to know. She pictured his face as the phone rang and her thumbnail photo swam up, indicating it was her: he would smile though he was alone. He'd be interested in her strange meetings. She did walk through the valley and he accompanied her, and he would be happy about her talking with Cate Crawley in a way that even she, flustered, was not.

Cate lifted her phone out of the bag, staring at the bag for a few seconds. It was black calfskin with a pair of leather eyes tufted with green fake-fur brows on the outside. A Fendi trademark but really, five thousand dollars for *Sesame Street*? She was already sick of it and would probably pass it along to Holly. She thought of the black-haired woman who'd just slipped out of her room. How it would surprise her that Cate could take a new five-thousand-dollar purse and kick it down to someone else, or—more likely—forget it in a closet.

Some days Cate wanted to recapture the feeling inside, the warm slow-moving adrenaline soak, of suddenly having money. So much more than enough. She'd grown numb to that, and while she could still recall having the feeling of abundance early in her career, she couldn't *feel* it anymore.

She pressed with the pad of her forefinger the number one, J's phone. She like J had many cell phones, different numbers she gave out to people depending on the degree of their closeness to her, though each number she assured people was her most private and personal one. Cate's deepest number reached out to J's deepest number and set it singing, his own voice playing the hook in a song of his, *did you know you can call me? Did you know you can call me anytime?*

"I'll come home tomorrow," she said, "lay low," and hung up, feeling like another thought lay in the back of her throat, hiding. She pictured the woman who'd just left with the husband she'd met on the morning show: not at all a match, a slim bent elegance paired with a jowly absorption. What did people think of her with J, though, her fixedness beside his open, responsive face? She thought of his chest, the spit curls like the occasional bloom in an open field. Her distance from him made him seem achingly real. As real as her power, a sudden thing she felt lying like stripes across her waist, right where the woman's touch had been. If she touched it back it would, like any tattoo, pierce her. Pierce her through the static skin, through the time and place where she stood: new laws; a new set of propositions.

Author's Note

In this book my characters exist, at a deep level, in the world of physics. They are entangled and even when apart their movements shape and change one another's. They are also in superposition—never quite in a definable place and time. While superposition and entanglement are well established in physics, phenomena like the meaning of the double-slit experiment can be interpreted in different ways, though the one given here is a common one.

Acknowledgments

A portion of Fan's story was published in the novella *Stolen Moments*, published by Shebooks.

As always, the love and support of my husband Bruce Beasley, always my first, best reader, and of my son Jin Beasley, have made every creative act of mine possible.

Thanks also to Carol Guess, who has shown me what fiction can do, and who read an earlier version of this manuscript. Thanks to Brenda Miller, Kathryn Trueblood, Thor Hansen, and Sara Stamey for their support in life and work. A big shout-out to Chris Paola, for his love and his quantum help. Finally, a big thanks to Gregory Wolfe and Suzanne Wolfe, for believing in this story.

This book was set in Warnock Pro, designed by Robert Slimbach and named in honor of the co-founder of Adobe Systems, John Warnock. With this typeface Slimbach chose a deliberately eclectic approach, blending the traditional and the modern, to better represent the achievement of the man for whom the typeface is named.

This book was designed by Shannon Carter, Ian Creeger, and Gregory Wolfe. It was published in hardcover, paperback, and electronic formats by Wipf and Stock Publishers, Eugene, Oregon.